The Boy's Guide to the Historical Adventures of G. A. Henty

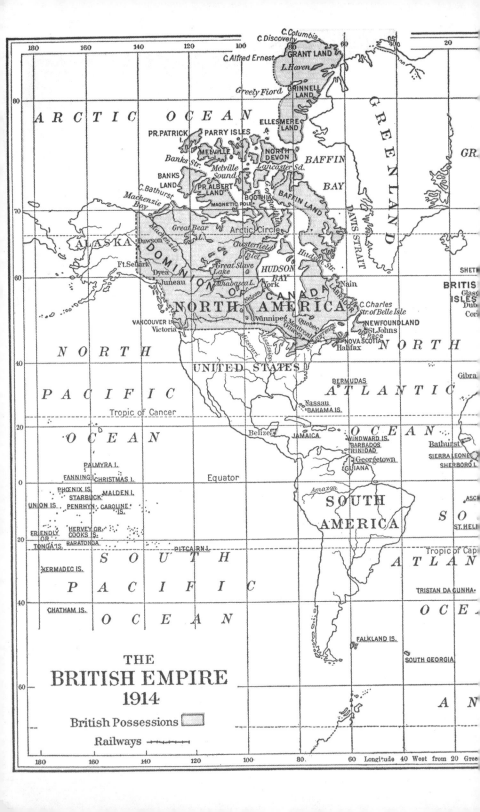

THE
BRITISH EMPIRE
1914

British Possessions
Railways

The Boy's Guide to the Historical Adventures of G.A. Henty

by William Potter

G.A. Henty

THE VISION FORUM, INC.

THIRD PRINTING
Copyright © 2000-2005 The Vision Forum, Inc.
All Rights Reserved

"Where there is no vision, the people perish."

THE VISION FORUM, INC.
4719 Blanco Rd., San Antonio, Texas 78212
1-800-440-0022
www.visionforum.com

ISBN-10 1-929241-15-1
ISBN-13 978-1-929241-15-6

Cover Design and Typesetting by Joshua R. Goforth

Detail of "Scotland Forever!", 1881, by Lady Butler (Elizabeth
Southerden Thompson, 1846-1933). Oil on canvas, 40 x 76 ½ in.,
Leeds Museums and Galleries (City Art Gallery), U.K.

Vision Forum is the home of the
All-American Boy's Adventure Catalog

PRINTED IN THE UNITED STATES OF AMERICA

For Brandon, Davis, and Jackson

May you always serve with honor and courage

Contents

Indian Troubles and Neighbors' Wars

The Victorian Era: Defending an Empire

PREFACE

E veryone loves a story well told. Consequently, it was
not surprising when, several years ago, our release
of *For the Temple*, by George Alfred Henty caused such a
stir. At the time, very few people knew of Mr. Henty. The
work of this prolific author had virtually vanished. This
fact is amazing when one considers that Mr. Henty's books
had influenced so many individuals, on several continents,
and were enjoyed by people from across a fairly wide
ideological spectrum. His work was acknowledged by
Nobel Prize winners, authors, historians, prime ministers,
generals, admirals, and other notables.

Although Mr. Henty was a well-known public figure
in his day, he never sought public approval or acclaim.
His simple motivation was to do his duty to God, family,
and country. On one occasion, a young admirer earnestly
asked Mr. Henty for his autograph. The autograph
was refused, not out of any vanity or imperiousness,
but as a result of Mr. Henty's deeply held belief that
young people should not be seeking the autographs of
so-called important public figures. This sounds almost
incomprehensible in light of today's self-promoting, self-

aggrandizing celebrities. Mr. Henty was more concerned about the character and the training of the young people reading his works. Essentially, he was telling this young autograph seeker, "You, and what you do with your life, are more important than an autograph."

The following excerpt from an interview with Mr. Henty—possibly his last—summarizes his beliefs:

> *To be a true hero you must be a true Christian. To sum up, then, heroism is largely based upon two qualities— truthfulness and unselfishness, a readiness to put one's own pleasure aside for that of others, to be courteous to all, kind to those younger than yourself, helpful to your parents, even if that helpfulness demands some slight sacrifice of your own pleasure. You must remember that these two qualities are true signs of Christian heroism. If one is to be a true Christian, one must be a Christian hero. True heroism is inseparable from true Christianity, and as a step towards the former I would urge most strongly and urgently the practice of the latter.*

I am grateful for the publication of *The Boy's Guide to the Historical Adventures of G.A. Henty* because I believe that it is critical that today's readers have a Christian framework for reading and understanding the rich legacy which Mr. Henty left to the boys of the world.

Doug Schmitt
President, Preston Speed
Mill Hall, Pennsylvania

Publisher's Introduction

Once upon a time, boyhood was a special season in a man's life when he could dream noble dreams and prepare for manhood. Today, the very concept of nobility and preparation have become passé with most young men. I suspect, however, that you are not like most young men. If you are holding this book and are reading this introduction, then it is a fair assumption that you care about the heroes and histories of the past. Somewhere along the way, you decided to turn off the television and pick up a book. Perhaps your parents introduced you to the joy of history and the remarkable works of Mr. G.A. Henty. However you arrived at this point, I want to strongly encourage you. With every page you read of Mr. Henty's literature, you are making a wise investment in your future. This book was published to help you on that journey.

The Boy's Guide to the Historical Adventures of G.A. Henty offers several unique features. First, it provides an overview of the remarkable life of George Alfred Henty. You will be delighted to learn that Mr. Henty was not only the foremost chronicler of history for boys, but he was an active participant in some of the more remarkable events of the 19th century. When you peruse a Henty novel, you are reading the words of a man who has tramped through the jungle with explorers, who has felt the sting of battle, who has celebrated victory and suffered defeat. What a contrast to the armchair historians of our generation.

Second, *The Boy's Guide* presents the reader with a sound, biblical basis for the study of history. Sir Winston Churchill once wrote that "the greatest advancements in human civilization have come when we recovered what we had lost: when we learned the lessons of history." To the extent that our generation has rejected the past, we have condemned our future. It is up to you to reverse this trend and reclaim the chivalric legacy of bold manhood once a hallmark of Western civilization. This is precisely why the writings of Mr. Henty are so important. Henty provides the young reader with a Christian framework for understanding more than 2,500 years of earth history.

Third, *The Boy's Guide* organizes the work of Mr. Henty chronologically by historical epoch and by the actual year of the event described in each book. We have divided Henty's books into eight epochs of earth history: "The Ancient World"; "The Middle Ages"; "Reformation and Colonization"; "Wars of Religion and Succession"; "Colonial Disruptions and Competition"; "The Napoleonic Era"; "Indian Troubles and Neighbors' Wars"; and "The Victorian Era."

There are a total of 72 books reviewed by the author in *The Boy's Guide*. This number represents all of the historical fiction books specifically written by Mr. Henty for boys. Mr. Henty did write other books including several histories and numerous works of pure fiction. He also wrote two books for girls. What makes the historical novels unique is their plot settings in the midst of genuine historical events and the interaction of the characters with actual men and women who shaped history. If you are already a true Henty aficionado, you may have discovered that, while there were only about 70 historical fiction adventures written for boys, many of these volumes were later published under different titles. To minimize confusion, we have decided to review and delineate the books based on their original titles as published by Blackie & Sons more than a century ago.

A fourth benefit of the book in your hands is that it provides you with both the historical background and a plot summary for each of Henty's novels. This will allow you to key your Henty readings with the rest of your academic studies. You will know, for example, that *The Cat of Bubastes* should be read in conjunction with your study of Egypt, that *Beric the Briton* would be a helpful tool for those studying early church history, or that *In Freedom's Cause* will compliment your readings on the history of England and Scotland. The plot summaries provide a helpful overview of the story line, and reveal insights into the moral issues which confront the young protagonists of each novel.

The next time you stumble across an obscure Henty in some antiquarian book shop, or even read of a new release from the publishers at Preston Speed, you will be able to consult *The Boy's Guide* and know in advance about the contents of the glorious treasures which lie before you.

Douglas Phillips
President, The Vision Forum, Inc.
Bulverde, Texas

Kudos Antiqua

"Mr. Henty is the king of storytellers for boys."
—*Sword and Trowel*

"Surely Mr. Henty should understand boys'
taste better than any man living."
—*The Times*

"Mr. Henty might with entire propriety be called
the boys' Sir Walter Scott."
—*Philadelphia Press*

"The brightest of the living writers whose office
it is to enchant the boys."
—*Christian Leader*

Why Boys Should Read the Magnificent Adventures of G.A. Henty

George Alfred Henty is a name that, 100 years ago, would have evoked instant recognition in the minds of millions as the author of adventure books for boys. Estimates of the number of his published works have ranged up to 25 million! Upon his death in 1902, the *London Sketch* wrote that "the boys of England lose one of the best friends they ever had."

One Henty scholar, Leonard R.N. Ashley, observed that "he wrote before adventure writing went into the areas of espionage and high technology and battles fought in galaxies far away. . . . His work was cherished [and] admired not only by boys but by parents who were pleased that their children were growing up right under the tutelage of reliable patriotic teachers such as Henty." His historical fiction for boys was still being used up until the 1960s for the study of history in English schools.

The thrill of bold action and brave deeds by boys of Christian character and fortitude captured the imaginations of young men around the world. Beautiful authorized editions of Henty rolled off the presses of Blackie & Sons of London and Edinburgh and Scribners in New York;

cheap binderies in New York and Philadelphia flooded the American market with pirated editions.

Henty's boyish heroes reminded the young men of Britain and the United States of the goals of Lord Tennyson's Ulysses–"to strive, to seek, to find, and not to yield."

A LEGACY OF BOLD MANHOOD

Who was G.A. Henty? How did this remarkable man teach history to so many boys and at the same time instill in them a desire to be like his heroes—stalwart, self sufficient, responsible, and addicted to duty faithfully performed? And why have so few people today heard of Henty except as a footnote in Victorian children's literature? He received only a brief paragraph in the *Cambridge Biographical Dictionary*.

The answer to the last question becomes obvious upon reading your first Henty book. His stories are full of self-disciplined and honorable men: protective of women, fearless in battle, defenders of the British Empire, scornful of compromising principle. To the modern mind, Henty is dangerous—patriarchal, sexist, imperialistic. Henty's heroes do not fit the mold of contemporary children's fiction. As one critic recently noted in a British magazine article about G.A. Henty:

> *Most of today's children's books are populated by prissy paragons, of indeterminate sex, who spend their lives working in shelters for the homeless, lamenting the fate of native Americans and questioning gender stereotypes. In one book, a boy defies teasing to remain in a ballet class, in another, "lame teenager Shem"*

finds manhood "with the help of an old Indian woman" (*The Economist*, December, 1999).

The historical tales of George Alfred Henty promote manliness, self-reliance, and courage of conviction. With death on every hand, his men fight to the finish as Britons against Roman invasion, as Huguenots suffering persecution in France, as soldiers of England in many battles of empire throughout history. Note this description of battle at Poitiers in 1356 from *St.*

George for England:

> *D'Alencon appeared upon a rising ground on the flank of the archers of the Black Prince, and thus, avoiding their arrows, charged down with his cavalry upon the 800 men-at-arms gathered around the Black Prince, while the Count of Flanders attacked on the other flank.*
>
> *Nobly did the flower of English chivalry withstand the shock of the French, and the prince himself and the highest nobles and simple men-at-arms fought side by side. None gave way a foot. In vain the French, with impetuous charges, strove to break through the mass of steel. The spear-heads were cleft off with sword and battle-axe, and again and again men and horses recoiled from the unbroken line. Each time the French retired the English ranks were formed anew, and as attack followed attack a pile of dead rose around them.*

No ballet instructor or old Indian woman there. The stunning realism of danger and combat in Henty's stories did not spring from an uninformed literary imagination but from the personal experiences of one of the most remarkable and prolific characters of adventure and historical writing in the English-speaking world.

THE WORLD OF G.A. HENTY

The years of G.A. Henty, 1832-1902, coincide almost exactly with the reign of Queen Victoria in England. Born to a family of "comfortable" means, Henty was instilled with the values of the typical public school boy as he endured the hard life of the Westminster School in London for five years (age 14-18). He matriculated at Caius College, Cambridge, where he found, after a year in that institution, that it "did not teach what he needed to learn to live the life he wanted."

Apparently desirous of taking the Queen's shilling and perhaps finding adventure in the almost limitless opportunities of the world's greatest empire, George's father purchased for his son a lieutenant's commission in the purveyors department of the army commissariat. As a stock-broker and coal-mine owner, he probably could not afford the £450 necessary for a captaincy in a line regiment (£1,300 in a Guards Regiment), much less the £4,500 for a Lt. Colonelcy (£9,000 for the Guards!).

Lt. Henty served in the hospital commissariat in the Crimean War at the notorious Scutari base. He witnessed the horrors and heroes of battle for the first time and was attracted to them like a moth to a flame. The young officer came out of the campaign with a Turkish Order of Merit "for his own reckless performance in battle" (Ashley, p. 31). The Crimean War took the lives of about 4,000 British soldiers in battle but about 15,500 from sickness. Henty's service in the pest-hole of Scutari took the life of his brother who died of cholera and resulted in George's evacuation home suffering with enteric fever. Henty's vicissitudes in the army made him a "lifelong critic of military ineptitude" but confirmed his belief that "military experience was beneficial to the individual as well as the nation" (Ibid., p. 38).

After service in Belfast and Italy and promotion to captain, G.A. Henty resigned his commission and joined the colorful but dangerous profession of war correspondent. He had sent accounts of the Crimean fighting to London newspapers while in the service and demonstrated real aptitude for writing with accuracy and clarity. His patriotism shone through his dispatches and the opportunity to go wherever war and danger afforded was a temptation too exciting to resist. Now in the employ of the *Morning Advertiser* and *The Standard*, Henty followed the sound of the guns wherever they led.

Over six feet tall and more than 240 pounds and sporting a ferocious patriarchal beard, George Henty was not a man to be trifled with. He could walk 50 miles in a day and was a formidable boxer and wrestler. Set upon by four knife-wielding bandits in Italy, Henty disarmed them all and sent them flying. An Irishman insulted his wife on a street in Belfast and Henty beat him to the ground. He fought a duel with a Spaniard who insulted Queen Victoria. Cultivation of personal honor, manly independence, and tenacity were character traits of George Henty and he instilled them in his boys of literary fiction and through those characters to his youthful readers.

The greatest dangers ex-captain-of-the-commissariat Henty encountered were in military campaigns of the 19th century. He joined the soldier of fortune and great Italian patriot Garibaldi in 1864. In the Italian-Austrian War, correspondent Henty traveled in disguise to get close to the action and came close to being shot as a spy. Where others shied away, Henty pressed forward. He joined the explorer-adventurer and fellow correspondent, Henry Morton Stanley aboard his boat *The Dauntless* and traveled down the coast of Africa and up the Volta River to join the British expedition against the Ashantees. Both Stanley and Henty fought in the Battle of Coomassie where Henty fought hand-to-hand with Ashantee warriors and Stanley "plied the most daring enemy with a never-failing aim." As Leonard Ashley has observed, no officer of the British army participated in all three wars: the Crimean, Abyssinian, and Ashantee Wars—but G.A. Henty was there for all of them. The adventurous correspondent was not satisfied with just writing about history, he became a part of it.

Throughout all of his adventures, G.A. Henty was unconsciously stocking his memory with the raw material for books he would write in the future. At the age of 36, a providential bout of ill-health forced Henty to stay home where his rich frame-of-reference, writing skills, love of history, fertile imagination, and Victorian values all came together for the benefit of English-speaking boys.

After writing several novels of indifferent success, G.A. Henty in 1871 wrote an adventure story expressly for boys. Entitled *Out on the Pampas*, the story was set in South America and proved a commercial success, launching his career as a writer of books for boys. A unique feature of that first book was his use of his children's names for the main characters.

Henty's marriage to Elizabeth Finucane had produced four children, two boys and two girls. His wife died in 1865 before the age of 30 and both Maud and Ethel died in their teens. Very little is known of Henty's son Herbert, but his eldest son Charles lived to maturity, served in the

Irish Fusiliers, and tried to continue his father's work after his death in 1902.

A number of titles appeared in the 1870s, several based on his own experiences in the Franco-Prussian War (*The Young Franc-Tireurs*) and others relating to specific historical conflicts like the Peninsula War between Napoleon and Wellington (*The Young Buglers*) and the Wars of Marlborough (*The Cornet of Horse*). His reputation was secure and for 30 years the books of George Alfred Henty were avidly read and his name became a household word.

Many stories in the G.A. Henty books took place within the context of the 19th century British armies. The sun never did set on the British Empire and those territories and peoples had to be defended across the globe. The people of that century witnessed wars of empire in Europe, Africa, and Asia, and each of those conflicts were met by one of several armies flying the English banner.

In addition to the regular army, for instance, there existed three Indian armies (until 1895): Madras, Bombay, and Bengal. Prior to the Great Mutiny of 1857-59, covered by Henty in *Rujub the Juggler* and *In Times of Peril*, those armies were the private property of a chartered commercial company, The Honorable East India Company. Those forces were not, strictly speaking, part of the army of the Crown, although individual red and later khaki-coated regulars were available for rent to the Indian government or The Company.

The British army itself was commanded by idiosyncratic generals whose political overseers represented a hodgepodge of independent government departments whose interactions were sometimes unconnected and sometimes absolutely byzantine. Commissions were purchased (as Henty himself had done), and "generals sent to fight a campaign usually selected their staffs from among pleasant aristocrats." The army of the Crown "tolerated its eccentrics and regarded eccentricities as normal" (*Mr. Kipling's Army*, Byron Farwell, pp. 17,18).

As complex and difficult as the administration of the empire seemed, and though the army was sometimes fraught with incompetence, pettiness, and cruelty, the valor and discipline of the British soldier was legendary. The image of the red-coated line standing against overwhelming odds until victorious or annihilated has stirred the blood of many a boy over the past 200 years.

Valor, manliness, discipline, obedience, Christian civilization—all are ideas which today provoke charges of archaic paternalism or elicit declamations of disgust or revulsion, but they were the heart and soul characteristics of many of the men of the Victorian era.

The British ethos of war was established by the army's relationship to the British cultural, social, and political order. Byron Farwell has said of that army that "[they] lived by a system now despised, adhered to a set of attitudes and beliefs now mocked, and entertained a view of the world now thought amusing" (Ibid., p. 13). In the culture and, by extension, the army, the Victorian worldview defined the core of belief animating G.A. Henty, and he instilled the old values in the boy-heroes of his stories.

THE IMPORTANCE OF HISTORY

There are several very good reasons why boys should read the Henty historical novels. The first one relates to the undisguised appreciation of and interest in the study of history that his books promote and encourage.

The great reformer Martin Luther said that "historians are the most useful people and the best teachers, and they cannot be sufficiently honored, praised, and thanked." George Henty was first and foremost an historian, and he was honored, praised, and thanked as much as any historian of his generation and for a hundred years. He would have agreed that a people who do not know where they came from or who they are or know of the deeds of their fathers, often find it difficult to preserve the goodness of their society and plan their future.

The Old Testament provides a rich example of that principle: Jehovah commanded the children of Israel to read publically, every year, the history of their deliverance from Egyptian slavery and divine protection in the wilderness. They were to remember that their God was the God of history and that recounting His mighty acts in every generation reminded them that He was the central focus of their national identity, the sole object of their worship, and the fountainhead of their ethical character. When the Jewish historians failed in their tasks, the people forgot and they foundered as a nation.

Certainly, the English boys of the Victorian era learned at an early age, through G.A. Henty, Rudyard Kipling, and others, that their country was special, their national character benefited from a Christian heritage through Church and common law, and that their lives were well spent in defending their civilization. Henty chose numerous historic events from many nations and told stories with well-researched accuracy and appreciation. His thrilling tales, described in such rich detail, inspired some boys to civil service and Her Majesty's armed forces and some Henty readers later became internationally respected scholars in the English-speaking world. In fact, some achieved true greatness in their profession. A.J.P. Taylor, author of the acclaimed *Origins of the Second World War*, claimed Henty as his childhood favorite author and "provided witness of the accuracy of Henty's historical writing" (Henty Society Bulletin, #89). The renowned historian Arthur M. Schlesinger in his autobiography claimed that the acquisition of a new Henty book was a red-letter day. He recorded that "a man seldom knows just what causes him to choose his life's career, but I do not doubt that in my case this love of Henty was one formative influence"—high praise indeed!

A boy needs to love and appreciate history, and Henty's colorful and exciting prose set in real historical context can be one means of accomplishing that goal. Because the novels usually follow the life of one boy, various important historical characters and events pass in and out of the story and pique interest in further research after the novel is completed. For instance, in *On St. Bartholomew's Eve*, the reader is introduced to the great Christian Admiral, Gaspard de Coligny. How did he rise to prominence? Why did French Protestants flock to his banners? Why did the court fear his influence? Those kinds of questions naturally arise in the story and must be answered through further research on the Huguenots. Seeking more information on the Reformed Christians of France, a boy discovers that thousands of them fled to America and had positive influence in the British colonies far beyond their own small communities. The dedication to the Huguenot Society at the beginning of the Preston

Speed edition ought to inspire further interest in the amazing story of the faith and perseverance of the French Calvinists.

Some books elicit follow-up interest in studying primary sources—those letters, diaries, and journals kept by the participants in wars and battles chronicled by Henty. *With Lee in Virginia* could lead to dozens of interesting private accounts by participants in the campaigns of the Army of Northern Virginia. *With Clive in India, For Name and Fame, Jack Archer*, and other titles could lead to the study of works like *Marching to the Sound of the Drums* by Ian Knight (1999) which describes "the face of battle" in reminiscences of private soldiers in the major campaigns of the Victorian era, "From the Kabul Massacre to the Siege of Mafikeng."

Just as the movie "Gettysburg" and the Ken Burn's documentary "The Civil War" sparked a resurgent interest in studying the American War Between the States, so Henty provokes a hunger to know more of world history. Central to that history was the pursuit of war which has characterized mankind from the beginning of time and has shaped the course of all the peoples of every continent. In our own time, the wars of the 20th century have brought about the deaths of tens of millions of people, redrawn the maps of nations, and created the modern world. G.A. Henty realized the importance of national conflicts and he used them as the stage to bring out the excellent personal character of his heroes.

In many Henty stories, the hero literally covers a lot of ground. A boy who pays attention will learn historical geography in a non-academic environment and a window on the world will be opened. For instance, Beric the Britain lives, travels, and battles in a number of historic English sites but also takes ships to Gaul and Italy, traversing and describing the wonders of ancient Rome and the Apennines. The avid boy reader of Henty will come to know the location of Abyssinia, Kabul, Coomassie, and Peking. He will learn something of the culture of the Ashantees of Africa, the Maoris of New Zealand, and the Boers of the Transvaal. He will travel in his imagination with Sir Francis Drake around the globe and march the hot dusty trail with General Roberts through the Khyber Pass. He will take aim down the muzzle of his Enfield rifle in the ranks of the thin red line as the Russian Cavalry thunders down upon him or the Dervishes hurl their screaming masses across the sands of the Sudan. Whether the hero is in a scrap in India, Russia, the Middle East, or China, the Henty reader would do well to keep a world atlas nearby.

BUILDING COURAGEOUS BOYS

Perhaps the best reason boys should read G.A. Henty has already been alluded to: the Christian character of Henty's boy-heroes made them men of honor, fortitude, and perseverence. They took their place as leaders in the army, in civil government, in their professions, in trade, and in their families. They became manly men, unwavering in principle, eager to defend their families and prepared to die for family, nation, comrades, or in a just cause. Many of the real historical characters that anchor the stories, though flawed as all men are, still set examples that did not disappoint the boys of the story. From Richard the Lionhearted to William Wallace, from King Alfred to Gustavus Adolphus, from "Chinese" Gordon to the Duke of Wellington, we see examples of men devoted to duty, unafraid of death, makers of history. Are these not traits we want our boys to admire and embrace?

The values espoused by Captain Henty can be seen in the titles of a number of his books: *Do Your Duty, No Surrender, True to the Old Flag, Bravest of the Brave, By Sheer Pluck.* He often personally addressed his readers in the preface so the lessons of the story would not be missed and so that their appetites would be whetted for action. In *St. George for England* he wrote:

My Dear Lads,

You may be told perhaps that there is no good to be obtained from tales of fighting and bloodshed,—that there is no moral to be drawn from such histories. Believe it not. War has its lessons as well as Peace. You will learn from tales like this that determination and enthusiasm can accomplish marvels, that true courage is generally accompanied by magnanimity and gentleness, and that if not in itself the very highest of virtues, it is the parent of almost all the others, since but few of them can be practiced without it. The courage of our forefathers has created the greatest empire in the world around a small and it itself insignificant island; if this empire is ever lost, it will be by the cowardice of their descendants.

A COMPREHENSIVE GUIDE TO
HENTY'S BOYS LITERATURE

G.A. Henty was a prolific author, publishing some 30 adventure stories, several adult novels, and more than 70 historical novels for boys. While most of them can be read with enjoyment, we have concentrated on the works that were written specifically for boys and that revolve around sound historical events and characters. Some of the books were published under different titles in the United States and Great Britain and we have tried to cite those that are redundant without repeating the review. Also, some Henty titles were actually short stories stretched out and we have not reviewed most of those.

While many of the specific historical situations are probably unknown to most readers and the Victorian cultural context in which Henty wrote is buried in archives more than 100 years old, the values he taught through his characters have no historical boundaries: honor, courage, manliness, gentleness, perseverance, patriotism, chivalry, respect, self-discipline, and service.

ANCIENT
HISTORY

---- ✠ ----

1250 B.C. - A.D. 70

THE CAT OF BUBASTES

A Story of Ancient Egypt (1250 B.C.)

Henty immersed himself in the historical records of many nations and times. This book is the first in chronology of Henty's tales, circa 1250 B.C. Egypt dominated the ancient world for centuries and Henty gives his young readers unsurpassed insight into the domestic life, customs, religion, and military system of that ancient kingdom.

Amuba, a prince of the Rebu nation on the shores of the Caspian sea, is carried with his charioteer Jethro into slavery after losing a vicious battle with the Egyptians. They become inmates of the house of Ameres, the Egyptian high priest, and are happy in his service until the priest's son accidentally kills the sacred cat of Bubastes. In an outburst of popular fury Ameres is killed, and it rests with Jethro and Amuba to secure the escape of the high priest's son and daughter. After many dangers they succeed in crossing the desert to the Red Sea, and eventually make their way back to the Caspian Sea and freedom.

THE YOUNG CARTHAGINIAN

A *Story of the Times of Hannibal* (220 B.C.)

Boys will enjoy reading the history of the Punic Wars (circa 200s B.C.) and develop a keen appreciation of the merits of a contest that was at first a struggle for empire, and afterwards for existence, on the part of Carthage. Hannibal, a creative and skillful general, crossed the Alps using elephants, and defeated the Romans at Trebia, Lake Trasimenus, and Cannae, and all but took Rome. It would be difficult to find a more exciting setting for this historic tale of adventure.

The hero of the story is Malchus, a Carthaginian aristocrat, who gets mixed up in a plot which occasions his leaving Carthage to join Hannibal in Spain. He crosses the Alps with the army and fights the Romans with sword and spear, up close and personal, in each major battle. He escapes a dungeon in Carthage and the mines of Sardinia to, in the end, marry a Gaullish maiden and settle in Germany, out of reach of Roman vengeance.

BERIC THE BRITON

A Story of the Roman Invasion (A.D. 61-70)

A ncient Rome surpassed all other nations as conquerors and rulers of Europe and the Middle East. Their military legions, their efficient political organization, their cultural hegemony overcame all before them. The armies of the tribes of Briton were among those who fell before the legionnaires' cohesive tactics and irresistible engines of war. Local victories by the barbarians were short-lived and reprisals for violation of the Pax Romana were swift and fierce. The subjugated people who conformed to Roman law could live peaceable lives and serve in the Roman system, sometimes rising to citizenship and position in the empire.

This is the story of Beric, a boy-chief of a British tribe which joins in the insurrection led by the indomitable Queen Boadicea in A.D. 62. Leading the survivors, Beric continues the war against the Romans in the fen-country until he and some of his men are captured and sent to Rome. He is trained in the school of the gladiators and achieves fame by defeating a lion which was set upon a Christian girl in the coliseum. The Briton is rewarded by appointment to librarian in the palace of the morally depraved Emperor Nero. Beric escapes and leads a band of outlaws in the mountains of Calabria, defies the power of Rome, and eventually returns to Britain after the death of Nero. He becomes a Christian, marries a Roman girl, and assumes his Roman-approved role as the trusted chief of his tribe.

FOR THE TEMPLE

A Tale of the Fall of Jerusalem (circa A.D. 70)

The long prophesied fall of Jerusalem in A.D. 70 provides the setting for this unusual tale. Using the record of Flavius Josephus, the Jewish historian in the employ of the Romans who faithfully recorded the events of the day, Henty depicts the conflicts of politics, religion, and culture between the Jews and the Romans in the days of the revolt of Palestine against Rome. The destruction of the temple of Solomon and the slaughter and dispersion of the Jews under the persecution of Emperor Titus followed the failure of the rebellion, and the history of the world was changed forever.

A young Jewish boy named John passes from the vineyard to the service of Josephus to the leadership of a guerrilla band of patriots. He fights bravely in the siege of Jerusalem and after the destruction of the Temple serves a brief stint as a slave in Alexandria before gaining the favor of Titus and accepting the district governorship of Galilee. After coming in contact with an Essene-type community, John converts to Christianity. Henty's boys always land on their feet, even though they sometimes back a losing cause.

THE
MIDDLE
AGES

———— ✠ ————

870 - 1480

THE DRAGON AND THE RAVEN

Or, The Days of King Alfred (870-900)

The Saxons and the Danes fought fierce battles for supremacy in Britain in the eighth and ninth centuries. The Norsemen conquered East Anglia, crossed the Thames, and engaged the West Saxons in a series of battles in A.D. 871. In the midst of the struggle, 23-year-old Alfred ascended the tottering throne and temporarily beat back the pagan hordes and concluded a peace treaty, which proved temporary. Following another war in 878, peace was again achieved; the Danish King Guthrum accepted Christianity and withdrew to East Anglia, and Alfred the Great fortified the cities, built a navy, codified the laws, and revived learning among the Saxons until his death in A.D. 900.

The hero is a young Saxon thane named Edmund who joins the forces of King Alfred and fights the Danes on land and sea. Driven from his home, Edmund takes on the Vikings in their own element, the sea, in his ship *The Dragon*. The young Earldoman is carried by storms to the shores of Norway where he defeats Sweyn the Viking in single combat. Edmund takes part in the siege of Paris on behalf of the Franks and tracks down his nemesis in order to rescue the Danish maiden he will later marry before returning to England to rejoin Alfred.

WULF THE SAXON

A Story of the Norman Conquest (circa 1066)

The last days of Saxon England and the conquest of King Harold and his army by William of Normandy provide the colorful backdrop for one of Henty's most popular children's books. Harold had ruled England for less than a year when Norse invaders threatened from two directions at once. The Saxon king hurried north and crushed the Norwegian forces at Stamford bridge but suffered heavy losses himself. He then conducted a forced march of more than 300 miles to take on one of the finest armies in Europe led by the ablest captain of the age. The weakened Saxon forces were crushed at the Battle of Hastings, bringing Norman rule to England in the last successful invasion of that nation in history by a foreign power.

The hero is a young thane who wins the favor of Earl Harold and joins his retinue. When Harold becomes king, Wulf assists in the Welsh Wars and fights at Stamford Bridge against the Norsemen. In the mighty struggle at Hastings, Wulf stands with his king and fights valiantly to the end as Harold's thanes die around him and he is killed, allegedly from an arrow through the eye. Because of previous dealings with the new King William, Wulf is able to keep his estates and does his part to amalgamate the Normans by marrying a noble's daughter.

WINNING HIS SPURS

A Tale of the Crusades (1188-92)

Also published under the titles *The Boy Knight* and *Fighting the Saracens*, the theme of this book is the attempt of European Christendom to drive the Saracens from the Holy Land in the third Crusade. After the capture of Jerusalem by the Muslim leader Saladin, a coalition of Christian rulers led an expedition to recapture the "holy city." In the end, only King Richard, known as "the Lion-Hearted," completed the journey and faced his Islamic rival. Acre fell to the Christians thus securing a post for future exploits by the Knights of the Church but the Muslims retained their hold on Jerusalem. The Preston Speed edition of this book has a helpful introduction of historical and theological context by Byron Snapp.

The hero, Cuthbert, begins his story with an ambush of outlaws in a Worcestershire wood in which he kills a kidnapper with a crossbow arrow and rescues a little maiden. He enters the service of King Richard and makes the long journey to the Holy Land to war with the Saracens. With bows and battle-axes he fights his way across Europe and into the Middle East. In a last stand with his company in Palestine, Cuthbert is struck in the head by a Nubian wielding a mace and regains consciousness as a prisoner of the enemy. The intrepid boy escapes and faces dangerous adventures in the return trip across Europe. He is knighted for his heroic exploits and in due course aids in the rescue of King Richard in Austria and returns triumphant to England.

IN FREEDOM'S CAUSE

A Tale of Wallace and Bruce (1296-1314)

In 1296, Edward I, called Longshanks, stormed Berwick, massacred the whole town, then conquered the Scottish army of John Baliol, and proclaimed himself King of Scotland. The Scottish nobles acquiesced to his brutal and tactless rule. A capable and heroic leader named William Wallace led the people in a rebellion for freedom. Wallace's ragged army routed the English forces at Stirling Bridge, then carried the war into England. Edward returned home from the war in France and led his forces to victory over Wallace at Falkirk. In 1306, Robert the Bruce took up the sword which was stricken from Wallace's hand and claimed the crown of Scotland. Young, strong, aggressive, and persistent, King Robert battled the English for six years and in 1314 had a final showdown at Bannockburn. With only 10,000 men to the English 30,000, the Bruce wrecked the English host and secured the freedom and nationhood of Scotland.

Archie Forbes becomes the ardent follower of Wallace and forms a troop of scouts for the Scottish army. After Falkirk and Wallace's death, he aligns with Bruce. Adventures abound in the moors of Scotland as Archie's cold steel is bloodied in the cause for Scottish independence. He is able to reclaim his estates wrongfully taken by neighbors and he joins in the final victory at Bannockburn.

ST. GEORGE FOR ENGLAND

A Tale of Crecy and Poitiers (1340-56)

Two of the most resounding victories of English arms occurred at the beginning of the Hundred Years War with France. Edward III invaded France to lay claim to Gascony and secured the Flemish trade for English merchants. The 8,500 veteran troops of Edward were confronted by about 12,000 French soldiers at Crecy, and in the resulting battle, the English longbow men mowed down the French forces, killing upwards of 10,000. Ten years later, again greatly outnumbered, the English, this time led by Edward, the Black Prince, wrecked another French force, inflicting over 5,000 casualties. The enemy's crest was seized and taken to the princes of Wales as a trophy. The three white ostrich plumes and King John's motto Ich dien (I serve) on the crest "[was] the sort of motto of which Henty and his heroes thoroughly approved" (Ashley, p. 152).

The boy-hero of this tale is Walter Somers, a foundling who is reared by a blacksmith who also teaches him the use of a sword. Tall, strong, skilled, and brave, Walter, by a typical Hentyesque providence, meets the Prince of Wales and joins the invasion of Brittany and Flanders. He gives good account as they pile the French dead in front of their line of battle. Walter survives the black death and the Battle of Poitiers, and marries the girl he saved from pirates. This book packs more historical detail into the story than almost any other Henty title.

THE LION OF ST. MARK

A Tale of Venice in the Fourteenth Century (1380)

This is a story of Venice at a period when her strength and splendor were put to the severest tests. The merchant states of the Mediterranean vied for supremacy in the expanding trade upon which European rulers were becoming increasingly dependent.

The hero of this tale is Francis Hammond, son of an English merchant in Venice, who displays a fine sense of manliness and courage which carry him safely through an atmosphere of intrigue, crime, and bloodshed. In his gondola on the canals and lagunes, and in the ships which he rises to command, Hammond succeeds in extricating his friends and himself from imminent dangers, and contributes largely to the victories of the Venetians at Porto d'Anzo and Chioggia. He is honored by the state, and finally wins the hand of the daughter of one of the chief men of Venice. As he does in other volumes, Henty writes "of other empires and aims to point to morals from their history which were relevant to that of Britain" (Berlyne, p. 26).

A March on London

Wat Tyler's Rebellion (1381)

The poll-tax furnished the occasion for a wide-spread uprising of the peasants, beginning in East Anglia and Kent. The rebels from Kent followed a charismatic and aggressive leader named Wat Tyler against London. The revolt was violent but essentially unorganized as the farmers and laborers sought to "strike off the shackles of serfdom." They actually did strike off the heads of a few lawyers and terrorized landlords and royal officials and in the London riots, slew the Archbishop of Canterbury. In the end, the king agreed to some demands, Wat Tyler was killed, and the rebellion fell apart. A hundred or so leaders were executed for their part in the revolt.

The main character of the story is Edgar Ormskirk, the son of a scholar and scientist of Dartford. Edgar rejects following in his father's footsteps and moves to London where he risks life and limb to save the life of a wealthy merchant. There is plenty of action as the rebellion flows into the streets of London. The ill-treatment of the peasants and their just demands for relief are forcefully presented in Tyler's speeches. Our hero ends up in Flanders, so often tied to England's history, for further adventures.

BOTH SIDES OF THE BORDER

A *Tale of Hotspur and Glendower* (1400)

King Henry IV faced a number of rival claimants to the throne and rebellions against his authority. The most serious menace to his rule came from a Welsh aristocrat, Owen Glendower, who aroused the spirit of Welsh nationalism and formed alliances with the Scots, French, and rebellious English vassals. The Percy family, led by the Earl of Northumberland and his son "Harry the Hotspur," aligned themselves with Glendower and marched with their vassals to join him. The 17-year-old son of the king, also named Henry, swept down on the Percies and defeated them at Shrewsbury, killing young Hotspur and thus gaining a respite from challenges to the throne.

Oswald Forster, the son of a border chieftain, binds himself as a squire to young Hotspur. After an adventure in Scotland he eagerly joins Glendower's rebellion in Wales and helps the Welsh leader's daughters escape capture. His bold actions and success in fighting in Scotland bring him a knighthood and he is by the side of Hotspur at the Battle of Shrewsbury. After his lord's death, Oswald returns to the Scottish border with an unsullied reputation as a man of high moral character and unmatched skill at arms.

AT AGINCOURT

A Tale of the White Hoods of Paris (1415)

King Henry V renewed his claims to the French throne and invaded France determined to press his claim on the field of battle. John Keegan has best described the excitement of studying the clash in Flanders: "Agincourt is one of the most instantly and vividly visualized of all epic passages in English history. It is a victory of the weak over the strong, of the common soldier over the mounted knight, of resolution over bombast, of the desperate, cornered, and far from home, over the proprietorial and cocksure. It is an episode to quicken the interest of any schoolboy bored by a history lesson" (John Keegan, p. 79).

The English hero of this adventure story is Guy Aylmer, a redoubtable English squire, who confronts numerous obstacles in France. He defends his lord's castle but is later given up as a hostage and enters Paris while the city is in the midst of a typical Parisian upheaval—the butchers are in control! After negotiating several tight situations, Guy meets an exiled Italian count and his lovely daughter, and, of course, marries her. In the end, the hero of the tale ends up at Agincourt, one of the greatest victories of English arms.

A KNIGHT OF THE WHITE CROSS

A Tale of the Siege of Rhodes (1480)

The Order of the Knights of St. John had a long and storied history of defending the places declared holy by the Church and protecting pilgrims who traveled to those sites. Bound by vows of obedience, chastity, and poverty, they established the great Hospital, a guest house, in Jerusalem. The Knights Hospitallers, like the Templars, became a military order which established castles to defend against Moslem armies at Acre, then Crete, then the Island of Rhodes where they withstood two terrible sieges by the Turks. They obtained honorable terms from Soleiman the Magnificent and retreated to Malta where they successfully resisted every attempt of the Muslim invaders to destroy them.

The story begins during the War of the Roses in England, but the hero Gervase Trentham soon joins the Knights of St. John in Rhodes. A man dedicated to God's service and pious in his personal life, Gervase uncovers a plot and saves the coast of Italy from the Muslim corsairs and is knighted by the Grand Prior. After doing time in a Tripolitan dungeon, the English knight draws his sword in the bloody defense of Rhodes. He finds himself in a tough position desiring marriage but having taken a vow of chastity. In the end, it is the Roman pontiff that gives him the break he needs to wed.

REFORMATION
AND
EXPLORATION

✛

1579 - 1595

BY PIKE AND DYKE

A Tale of the Rise of the Dutch Republic (1579-85)

In the 16th century, the Protestant Netherlands fought a war of survival against the Duke of Alva and Phillip II's Spanish armies who sought to impose Roman Catholicism on the Reformed Church. And it was a noble struggle indeed—"Out of half-submerged morasses . . . a rational and conservative republic is slowly evolved—born amid blood and fire, but dilating daily through storms and darkness to more colossal proportions. From the handbreadth of territory called the province of Holland rises a power which wages eighty years warfare with the most potent empire upon earth" (Motley, p. III).

Henty traces the conflict through the adventures and brave deeds of an English boy in the household of the ablest man of his day—William the Silent. Edward Martin, the son of an English sea captain, enters the service of the Prince as a volunteer, and is employed by him in many dangerous and responsible missions, in the discharge of which he passes through the great sieges of Leiden and Harlaam. He ultimately settles down as Sir Edward Martin and becomes the husband of the lady to whom he owes his life, and whom he in turn had saved from the Council of Blood.

St. Bartholomew's Eve

A *Tale of the Huguenot Wars* (1570-72)

Some of the bitterest persecutions of the Counter-reformation were waged against the Reformed Protestants of France by the Roman Catholic Guise family and monarchs of the 16th and 17th centuries. Thousands of French Calvinists, known as Huguenots, were killed and thousands more fled to other European countries and the Americas. They made far-reaching cultural, political, and economic contributions wherever they went, but they paid a heavy price for their faithfulness to God. On August 24, 1572, the Parisian mobs, following the example of Catherine de Medici and the Guises who instigated the murder of the great Protestant Admiral Gaspard de Coligny, massacred more than 2,000 Protestant men, women, and children—the gutters overflowing with their blood. The massacre triggered persecutions across France and the volunteer soldiers of the Reformed Church were again forced to defend themselves against the onslaughts of the Catholic armies.

In this Henty tale, 16-year-old Phillip Fletcher, of English and French heritage, joins the forces of Admiral Coligny and Henry of Navarre to fight for religious freedom in France in the 1570s. He leads a squad of veteran soldiers against Catholic forces behind the battle lines, in sieges of castles and towns, and in defense of family estates. Ever fearless, Phillip uses his consummate skills as a swordsman and marksman in many desperate engagements, often hand-to-hand. He barely escapes the Paris massacre, rescues a noble lady, and returns to England as a hero, to experience matrimony and to claim his patrimony.

UNDER DRAKE'S FLAG

A Tale of the Spanish Main (1580)

Of all the freebooters who flew the English flag and raided Spanish shipping, none was more carefree, colorful, and dangerous than Sir Francis Drake. He was also the boldest and ablest seaman of his time and with his ship *The Golden Hind*, he eluded all pursuit on the high seas or closed in tight for the capture or the kill. Few adventure stories have ever exceeded the excitement and real-life drama of the privateers. Henty "portrays the sea-dog as more important than Shakespeare and all the scribblers of the Golden Age of Queen Elizabeth" (Ashley, p. 137).

The boy-hero who sails with Drake is Ned Hearne, a Devonshire lad. He embarks on the journey which carries Drake's crew around the world, with adventures aplenty on the Spanish Main. Ned and a companion are washed up on an island shore when their little prize ship breaks up in a storm. Taking to the woods, they lead the first successful insurrection against Spain in the western islands. The resourceful seamen elude capture and rejoin Drake's ship, only to fall, soon after, into the clutches of the Inquisition. Rescued again, Ned sails to the South Seas and finally to England where he collects his prize money and settles down until the Queen calls him out again. He soon joins in the defeat of the Spanish Armada which marks the beginning of the end of the Iberian's domination of the world's oceans.

By England's Aid

The Freeing of the Netherlands (1585-1604)

Henty crafts a distinctive plot following the exploits of two characters in his second work on the fight for Dutch freedom. England finally overtly assists the Low Countries in their war for Independence as brothers Geoffrey and Lionel Vickers fight in both theatres of the war—Lionel with the army in the battles of Nieuport, Ivry, and Ostend, and Geoffrey on the ocean. After many adventures, the sailing brother finds himself a prisoner aboard an enemy ship during the great defeat of the Spanish Armada, one of the most important battles in history. Geoffrey escapes, only to fall into the hands of the Corsairs. Saved by a wealthy Spanish merchant, he regains his native country after the capture of Cadiz, which finally broke the power of Spain in Europe. Both brothers marry well, one to a Spanish lady who becomes a Protestant and settles gladly in England, though she complains about the weather.

BY RIGHT OF CONQUEST

With Cortez in Mexico (1519-21)

The 16th century was the age of conquest in which European nations expanded their power around the globe. Spain led the way in Mexico where Hernando Cortez molded the template for triumph with his bloody campaign against the Aztec Empire. By the time the conquistador arrived, the Aztecs, led by Montezuma II, had subjugated most of Mexico and established an elaborate civilization which included many human sacrifices to their sun god. After one of the great sieges of history against the capital city of Tenochtitlan (Mexico City), Cortez with only several hundred Spanish soldiers and several thousand Indian allies destroyed the Aztec Empire and shipped the loot back to Spain.

The hero of the story is a shipwrecked Englishman named Roger Hawkshaw who combines a keen sense of adventure with intrepid perseverence in potentially fatal circumstances. He also possesses a fine facility with foreign languages which enables him to survive in the jungle among savage tribes and join up with Cortez in the overthrow of the Aztecs. In the end he escapes with plenty of treasure and marries an Indian princess. Henty pulls no punches in describing the barbarism of the Aztecs and the Spaniards.

WARS OF
RELIGION
AND SUCCESSION

✠

1630 - 1745

THE LION OF THE NORTH

A Tale of Gustavus Adolphus and the Wars of Religion (1618-48)

The Thirty Years War began in Bohemia with the Protestant revolt against Roman Catholic domination. The war went through four phases, the third being the entry into Germany of the Swedish King—the Lion of the North—Gustavus Adolphus. The Protestant champion led the most formidable military machine in Europe and for the first time, the Catholic forces under the experienced General Tilly and the soldier of fortune Wallenstein suffered shattering defeats and fell before the Swede's impassioned and disciplined veterans. Likened by historians to Alexander the Great, Adolphus animated his soldiers by example rather than rhetoric; he exceeded all others in tactics, organization, and arms, and drove the Catholic imperial army from the field at Brietenfeld and Lutzen, inflicting staggering losses. In the latter engagement, the Swedish King was killed in action, the result of which was the reckless fury of his army in completing the victory.

Scotsmen love a fight and Malcolm Greene is a Scotsman. He is recruited to fight for Sweden under the greatest soldier of the century, Gustavus Adolphus, and duly throws himself into the fray in the great battles of the first half of the Thirty Years War. In the disciplined ranks of the Scotch Brigade we meet Mackay, Hepburn, and Munro—heroes all and destined for greatness. Malcolm confronts rebellious peasants, goes "undercover" as a clockmaker, and in the end marries the lovely Thelka with whom he will live out his days on the moors of Scotland.

WON BY THE SWORD

A Tale of the Thirty Years War (1640s)

As he did in *Lion of the North*, Henty turned his attention to the wars of religion which involved all of Europe. The scene of this story is laid in France in what historians consider the fourth and last phase of the Thirty Years War. The main characters are the powerful and ruthless Cardinal Richelieu, chief minister of Louis XIII and the real ruler of France for 18 years; Cardinal Mazarin, the clever Italian assistant to Richelieu who never served as a priest, may have married the king's widow, and with amazing guile succeeded his master; and Anne of Austria, mother of the four-year-old king Louis XIV and Regent of the nation until Louis came of age.

The hero is a Scotsman, Hector Campbell, orphaned son of a Scotch officer in the French army. How he attracted the notice of Marshal Turenne and of the Prince of Conde, how he rose to the rank of Colonel, how he finally had to leave France pursued by the deadly hatred of the Duc de Beaufort—all these turns of events—are woven together as our Gallant fights several battles in France and Italy, engages in three duels, saves Mazarin's life, and finally settles peacefully in Berkshire.

FRIENDS THOUGH DIVIDED

A Tale of the Civil War (1642-60)

With the raising of the royal standard at Nottingham, the king initiated the English Civil War. Arrayed on one side were the men loyal to King Charles, known as Cavaliers. The men opposed to them were the supporters of Parliament, known as Roundheads. Lords and commoners fought on both sides, divisions often decided by religious belief. The Puritans who wanted continuing reformation of the English church sided with Parliament and those who desired a return to sacerdotal practices or at least a rollback of reformed influences on the church, backed the King's party. Charles Stuart was defeated and beheaded for treason and, under the leadership of Oliver Cromwell, the Parliamentarian forces ruled without a king until Charles II returned from exile in 1660.

Henty introduces young men representing each side of the struggle, Harry Furness and Herbert Rippinghall. The fortunes of Harry the Cavalier receive most of the attention, however, as the contending parties fight in England, Scotland, Ireland, and on the high seas. Harry is ever the gentleman and a man of complete honor, treating his enemies with respect, and defending his friends at every providential turn of events. He is captured at the siege of Drogheda and enslaved in Bermuda, but escapes to England. Following the fortunes of Charles II, Harry flees with the king to France and returns in 1660 to assume his place in the new royal order. Herbert fights honorably in the war and ends his days after the Restoration as a member of Parliament.

WHEN LONDON BURNED

A Story of the Plague and the Fire (1666)

Charles II was firmly on the throne of England in the time of the Restoration when the "Great Plague" carried off thousands of people in London in 1665, followed a year later by a fire which broke out in a baker's shop and spread from street to street through London until half the city was destroyed. The non-conformist Christians outside the Church of England viewed the disasters as God's judgment on the extravagant and licentious court and the wicked monarch.

Cyril Shenstone is a typical paragon of Henty's boy heroes: trustworthy, unselfish, and brave to a fault. He survives the plague, helps save people and their possessions in the midst of the fire, and ships aboard a fighting vessel to battle their Dutch enemies, new rivals for commercial ascendency around the world. An interesting feature of this story is Henty's sympathetic view of the English non-conformist Christians.

ORANGE AND GREEN

A Tale of the Boyne and Limerick (1690)

After William of Orange ascended the throne of England in the Glorious Revolution of 1688, the exiled James II made an attempt to regain a Catholic Stuart crown in Ireland where a rebellion led by Richard Talbot had temporarily overthrown English rule. He landed his forces in Cork in 1689 and with French and Irish allies laid siege to Londonderry, defended by the Scotch-Irish men loyal to William III. The king took to the field himself and inflicted a crushing defeat on the Irish army on the banks of the Boyne. James fled to France but the Irish continued the ferocious struggle for two more years until English victory and the signing of the treaty of Limerick.

Another pair of Henty heroes who are best friends—a Protestant, John Whitefoot, and a Catholic, Walter Davenant, find themselves on opposite sides in the troubles. Although they fight in their respective armies at Londonderry, the Battle of the Boyne, and other clashes of the rebellion, their good-will and mutual service are never interrupted. In the end the Davenants come into their own again and Walter marries a Protestant girl whom he had rescued. The boys exhibit religious tolerance in a land known for the opposite.

A JACOBITE EXILE

*Being the Adventures of a Young Englishman in the Service of
Charles XII of Sweden (1700-18)*

The most brilliant, daring, and erratic monarch of the early 18th century, Swedish King Charles XII, fought a prolonged conflict with the most ambitious, intellectually curious, and violent czar Russia had yet seen, Peter the Great. In 1700, Russia, Saxony, and Denmark made war on Sweden. Charles, the teenage monarch, defeated the Danes in one campaign, turned on the Russians and with 8,000 men routed the 40,000 men of the czar; and shortly thereafter disposed of the Saxon king. War continued with Russia and the others throughout his entire reign until the Swedish king was killed in battle in 1718 at the age of 36.

After the failure of two Jacobite rebellions in England, many of the defeated soldiers enlisted in the service of Scandinavian and Russian armies. Young Charlie Carstairs is a Jacobite forced to flee North Lancashire with his father and makes his way to Sweden. He distinguishes himself in several battles against the enemies of Sweden in northern Europe and Poland, and in the course of his adventures, meets both Charles XII and Peter the Great. Returning to England, he recovers his family estates and gives up the effort to reinstate the Stuarts.

THE CORNET OF HORSE

A Tale of Marlborough's Wars (1701-09)

England joined the Grand Alliance against France in the War of the Spanish Succession (known as Queen Anne's War in the American colonies). The conflict continued for about 12 years and was fought mostly in Spain, northern Italy, southern Germany, and the Spanish Netherlands. General Sir John Churchill, earl of Marlborough, was one of the greatest military geniuses of his age and he led the English forces throughout the war in the Netherlands. He won a number of brilliant victories against the French, one of the greatest at Blenheim where the French and Bavarian army of 50,000 suffered 50% casualties. Marlborough pursued the French to the end, defeating them at Ramillies, Oudenarde, Lille, and Malplaquet. As his descendant, Sir Winston Churchill said, "he never rode off any field except as a victor."

Rupert Holiday, a young man greatly influenced by both his grandfather and an exiled French aristocrat who teaches him fencing, is forced to flee England after injuring a miscreant in a fight. He joins the Duke of Marlborough's forces in the Low Countries and welcomes the combat so richly detailed by the author. This book is full of historical detail and it helped launch Henty's career as a writer of boys' novels, full of adventure and military prowess.

THE BRAVEST OF THE BRAVE

With Peterborough in Spain (1688-1707)

Henty again turned his attention to the war fought in Queen Anne's reign. The little known but remarkable and eccentric Charles Mordaunt, earl of Peterborough, served the Crown as admiral and general, diplomat and ambassador. He led English forces in the War of the Spanish Succession and in a remarkable siege captured Barcelona and installed an Austrian archduke as king of Spain. Henty states in his preface that Peterborough "showed a genius for warfare which has never been surpassed, and performed feats of daring worthy of taking their place among those of the leaders of chivalry."

Orphaned and ornery, Jack Stilwell begins life with two strikes against him. A frustrated uncle turns him over to an impressment gang and off he goes to Spain to join Peterborough. As an aide-de-camp to the general, he survives several adventures, faces down an angry mob bent on killing unarmed citizens, and helps the General in all the military actions in Spain. Jack also serves under Marlborough, exhibiting all the strength of character and valor expected of an English officer. This action-packed story ends with the former orphan a respected colonel and a member of Parliament.

IN THE IRISH BRIGADE

A Tale of War in Flanders and Spain (1710)

Prior to 1775, Catholics were not permitted to enlist in the English army. Irish regiments, however, served nobly and well on numerous occasions elsewhere. The Irish Brigade held an important place in the French army for over a hundred years, participating in battles across Flanders, Germany, Italy, and Spain. French generals testified to the extraordinary bravery of their Irish troops and they were conspicuous in every continental army. On many occasions they faced the hottest fire and greatest pressure in the War of the Spanish Succession.

The Irish hero of the tale is Desmond Kennedy, a man of unknown genealogy who enlists in O'Brien's Irish Brigade in service of Louis XIV. In Paris, he incurs the deadly hatred of a powerful courtier from whom he had rescued a kidnapped girl. He escapes one peril only to fall into another as he is captured in an attempted Jacobite invasion of Scotland. As an aide-de-camp to the duke of Berwick, Desmond has thrilling adventures in Flanders and is nearly murdered after a transfer to Spain. When peace returns to the continent, Captain Kennedy returns to Ireland to seek his patrimony and claim his estates.

BONNIE PRINCE CHARLIE

A Tale of Fontenoy and Culloden (1745)

In 1745 Prince Charles, the son of the exiled heir to the throne of James II—the last of the Stuart line but rejected in favor of the Hanoverian line of George II—secretly entered Scotland with a handful of followers to raise the clans and reclaim the thrones of Scotland and England. The Scottish followers of 'Bonnie Prince Charlie,' mostly highlanders, were known as Jacobites (after the Latin for James) and they flocked to his standard in kilt and war paint to fight the English army.

Henty's hero, Ronald Leslie, joins the rebellion in France and fights in the battles of Dettingen and Fontenoy and thereafter enlists in the uprising in Scotland. For a year, the Jacobites fight the English armies with some success, until the decisive Battle of Culloden. The clans who followed Charles onto that sanguinary field hurled a screaming attack at the enemy lines wielding their claymores and axes, but were cut down in bunches and virtually destroyed by the artillery fire and bayonets of the redcoats. The survivors and their families were harried from the land or killed. Ronald Leslie survives the disaster and makes his peace with His Majesty's government and returns to a quiet life in Scotland.

COLONIAL DISRUPTIONS AND COMPETITION

—— ✠ ——

1759 - 1786

WITH WOLFE IN CANADA

or The Winning of a Continent (1756-63)

The wars of empire between Britain and France encompassed several centuries and always spilled over into their colonial possessions. The Seven Years War (1750s, 60s) actually began in North America with an expedition led by a young Virginian named George Washington. England fared poorly in the first years of the war as French and Indian forces inflicted numerous defeats on poorly led and dispirited colonial and English armies. Change came with the appointment of the tenacious and brilliant William Pitt as Secretary of State, who took control of the war and appointed James Wolfe to command in America, a veteran general of proven strategic expertise and creative tactical ability.

The boy of the story, James Walsham of Sidmouth, suffers a succession of misfortunes—the death of his father, getting mixed up with smugglers, and succumbing to a military press gang. James always makes the most of a difficult situation, however, and becomes a fine soldier, eventually climbing the cliffs below Quebec with Wolfe's English forces and meeting the French army of General Montcalm on the Plains of Abraham for the decisive battle for the North American continent. Wolfe dies in the fight, but British arms achieve a stunning victory, the fruits of which double the size of the empire and lead, in a few short years, to a new war with the American colonies.

WITH FREDERICK THE GREAT

A Tale of the Seven Years War (1756-63)

Frederick the Great raised Prussia to the rank of a first-class power through the force of his personality, resolution, and military genius. In the Seven Years War, another international imbroglio in which England and Prussia formed an alliance against France and Austria, Frederick II had to hold off the forces of three empires which outnumbered the Prussians 12 to one. As an audacious tactician he defeated, *en seriatum*, France at Rossbach, the Austrians at Leuthen, and the Russians at Zorndorf. At Kunnersdorf in 1759 he was defeated by the combined forces of Austria and Russia but survived the debacle to conclude a favorable peace in 1763.

Fergus Drummond, yet another Scotsman who backed the Stuarts and ended up on the continent fighting someone else's war, seeks fortune and excitement and, to his credit, backs a winner in Frederick II. Fergus accepts the strict discipline and efficiency of the Teutonic army and through a combination of favorable providences and resolute deeds, he is promoted to colonel and serves on the King's staff. Twice captured, and twice escaped from Austrian fortresses, Fergus always performs valiantly, even saving Frederick's life in battle. In the end he marries a German heiress. This book is packed with historical detail.

TRUE TO THE OLD FLAG

A Tale of the American War of Independence (1776-81)

The American War for Independence (1776-1781) has, for most Americans, only one interpretation—that portrayed in the lurid prose of the Declaration of Independence: taxation without representation, oppression by the redcoats, the tyranny of King George III, etc. The compelling image of a united population of freedom-loving patriots has always held sway in American minds. The reality of the matter is that only one third of Americans supported the rebellion, about one third remained neutral, and the rest maintained loyalty to the Crown. Disregarding the minor discomforts of colonial status and loathing the violence of some of the rebels, outraged loyalists organized for the King. The war itself was a nearly-run thing and a large number of Americans gave good account against their fellow colonists.

The "Old Flag" of this Henty tale is the Union Jack of Britain and the point of view is that of a young Bostonian named Harold Wilson who leaves his adventures on the frontier to join his compatriots against the rebellion. Along the way he rescues several young girls from the Indians and exhibits the virtues of all the Henty heroes in desperate situations. This heroic boy is on the losing side this time and he flees to Canada after the war, with other Loyalists who remained true to the old flag.

HELD FAST FOR ENGLAND

A Tale of the Siege of Gibralter (1779-83)

This story deals with one of the most memorable sieges of history by the united forces of France and Spain. With land forces, fleets, and floating batteries, the combined resources of two great nations, they bombarded and besieged this grim British fortress in vain. "So long did siege of that rock last that a joke that became a catch phrase involved 'the anniversary of the siege of Gibralter' which meant any day of the year at all" (Ashley, p. 203).

Bob Repton is a fun-loving school boy who loves fun more than school and is removed by his guardian uncle and shipped to his sister's family to learn the wine trade in Gibralter. Bob, of course, takes a brave stand when the combined forces attempt to take The Rock. Before the long siege is over, it is apparent to all that Bob is a young man of cunning and tenacity, as is the English army defending the place. This was a hugely popular book and went through many editions.

WITH CLIVE IN INDIA

The Beginnings of an Empire (1751-86)

In 1751, Robert Clive rose to prominence in India, eventually providing the decisive leadership and real genius which resulted in Britain's making that country the crown jewel of her overseas empire. For three years he had been a clerk in the East India Company but upon joining the army, entered the field for which providence had unusually suited him. As a captain, he fought off the French and brought order to southern India. With an army of native Sepoys and the off-scourings of the London streets, Clive's little army of 3,000 men defeated a force of 50,000 Bengals at Plassey in 1757 and thus secured southern India for England.

Charlie Marryat goes to India as a writer with the East India Company. After escaping privateers and pirates, he lands safely in Madras to begin his work. Charlie meets Robert Clive, survives the siege of Arcot, and helps a friendly state defend against French attacks. Charlie endures the Black Hole of Calcutta and bravely throws himself into the fray at Plessey. In the end, Charlie returns home to England a hero, and lives out his days regaling his children with the stories of the great Clive of India.

THE NAPOLEONIC ERA

— ✠ —

1793 - 1815

IN THE REIGN OF TERROR

The Adventures of a Westminster Boy (1793)

The storming of the Bastille on July 14, 1789 signaled the beginning of the French Revolution. Within three years, the king was executed, and the following year a revolutionary tribunal was established to judge "enemies of the people." Led by Maximilian Robespierre, the Jacobins sought to establish a "Republic of Virtue" where all citizens would possess pure morals, high ideals, and unselfish patriotism. To achieve such virtue, the property of many nobles was seized and people accused of being anti-revolutionary were tried and sent to the guillotine (hence, "don't get shaved by the national razor"). Known as the Reign of Terror, everyone associated with the monarchy, anyone who expressed royalist views, and people who opposed the committee faced potential execution.

Harry Sandwith becomes a companion to the sons of a French aristocratic family and leaves England to join them. He wins the confidence of the family by saving their daughter from a mad dog. The Revolution takes its ugliest turn yet, and the Terror engulfs the whole family. Beset by perils, Harry becomes the protector of the three daughters at the house in his charge in Paris. After hair-breadth escapes they reach Nantes where the girls are condemned to death in the coffin-ships. Harry gives no thought to his own life to save the girls and the boy-protector gets them safely to England. He marries the youngest of the trio after completing medical training and following his father into the medical profession.

No Surrender!

The Story of the Revolt in La Vendee (1795)

The Vendee region of the French Province of Poitou erupted in revolt after the exacting of military levees and attempted destruction of the church by the Revolution. Led by their local priests and other community leaders, the army of Vendee defeated all the forces of the Republic that were thrown at them for 18 months. The very cause of their success—large peasant armies operating on home territory—proved their undoing when the farmers went home and the organized military might of the new government was unleashed on the region. The Great Terror came to the Vendee and more than 40,000 men, women, and children were butchered by the "Peoples' Army," their crops burned, the towns and homes razed, and churches destroyed.

The hero of the tale is Leigh Stansfield, an English lad drawn into the Vendee conflict while visiting his sister who is married to a French sea captain. He forms a company of scouts for the Vendean army and they fight with desperate valor many times over. Leigh's sister is condemned to the guillotine and he risks his own neck, traveling in disguise, to rescue her. The army is less and less successful and, as the revolt is ruthlessly crushed, the young Englishman escapes to England. The Vendee never surrendered.

A ROVING COMMISSION

Through the Black Insurrection at Hayti (1795)

In 1791, during the French Revolution, the slaves in Saint Domingue rebelled against their French masters, massacring many, destroying plantations, and looting towns. A brilliant leader and former slave named Toussaint L'Ouverture rose from among the revolutionaries and took control of the government. He played the various factions of French planters, government officials, international traders, and mixed race freedmen against each other to his own advantage. In 1799, Napoleon sent an army and hauled General L'Ouverture to prison in France but it was too late to reverse independence.

A British midshipman named Ned Glover on the West Indies Station is mauled by a wild dog as he rescues a French planter's daughter in Haiti. While he is on an operation against pirates, the slaves of Haiti rise up to throw off their French overseers and Ned is caught up in the rebellion and helps the French planter's family escape. Further exploits against Caribbean pirates give him opportunity to show his fighting skills and when war breaks out with France (who else?), he captures an enemy frigate.

THE TIGER OF MYSORE

The Story of the War With Tipoo Saib (1795)

One of the most colorful but black-hearted villains of India's history was the ruler of the sultanate of Mysore, Tipoo Sahib. The British Museum has a cleverly crafted toy which Tipoo had made for his amusement: a large tiger ripping apart a red-coated British soldier who emitted screams of terror, apparently to the delight of the sultan. Always conspiring against the English domination of India, he attacked neighboring territories when the Company was engaged elsewhere, and he conspired with the French to keep the English at bay. Richard Wellesley, Lord Mornington, was sent to Calcutta as governor-general and he quickly acquired the reputation of governing the subject peoples by "methods that were honorable and considerate as well as firm and just" (Larson, p. 607). Both the governor-general and his brother Arthur (later Lord Wellington), responded to Tipoo's perfidy by declaring war on Mysore in 1899 and laying siege to his capitol at Seringapatam, taking the city and killing the sultan.

This story is told through the life of Dick Holland, the son of a sea captain, and the daughter of an Indian Rajah. Dick grows up in England but returns to India in search of his ship-wrecked father, thought to be imprisoned by Tipoo Sahib. He rescues an English girl slave from the palace, finds his father, and through harrowing adventure, escapes the sultan's clutches. He is present at the assault on the palace and death of the tyrant and in typical Henty fashion, returns to England and marries the girl he rescued.

By Conduct and Courage

A Story of Nelson's Days (1795-97)

The success of the Royal Navy was the indispensable key to the protection and expansion of the British Empire. Dominant on the high seas for three centuries, the English fleets struck fear and commanded respect among all the nations of the world. No wonder so many of the Henty boy-heroes met their destiny aboard sailing ships. Napoleon's designs for the invasion of Britain and Ireland were ruined by Admiral Jervis when his fleet destroyed the Spanish fleet off Cape Saint Vincent and by Admiral Duncan who took nine of the 15 Dutch ships off Camperdown. Commodore Nelson displayed his amazing naval skills in that first encounter and would later be immortalized by his destruction of the French fleet at Trafalgar.

In this last Henty book, published after his death, Will Gilmore is brought up in a Yorkshire fishing village and enters the navy as a ship's boy. Within a few months he so distinguishes himself in action against the French that he is raised to the dignity of midshipman. His service in the West Indies Squadron brings command of a small cutter which he uses to chase down pirates. Will is a born leader of men, and his pluck, foresight, and calm resolve win him success where others have failed. After capture and escape three separate times, he is involved in the battles mentioned above and his final adventure involves a thrilling experience with no less a companion than Lord Nelson himself.

At Aboukir and Acre

A Story of Napoleon's Invasion of Egypt (1798)

Napoleon could never win a final victory while England controlled the sea. The French dictator embarked on a campaign to strike at English power in the Orient by invading Egypt in the summer of 1798. Admiral Nelson had been watching the French outside Toulon and promptly set out in search of the expedition, finding them at anchor in a bay near Alexandria. Nelson attacked in the evening and fought all night, leaving only four French ships not destroyed or captured. Napoleon was cut off from France and his designs on the Orient frustrated.

Edgar Blagrove is the son of an English merchant in Alexandria. His father leaves when the French fleet arrives and the boy is left behind. He links up with a Bedouin tribe and fights against the French in Cairo and at Acre when the enemy march into Palestine. Edgar witnesses the engagement at Aboukir, then joins the Royal Navy as a midshipman and becomes an interpreter for the commander. After the French are gone, he returns to Alexandria to run the family business and eventually returns to England.

AT THE POINT OF THE BAYONET

A Tale of the Mahratta War (1800-03)

This evocative title is the third of a dozen or so historical novels Henty placed in settings of the subcontinent. In 1804, the British made a treaty with the rulers of Gwalior. The peace and stability of the area was maintained until a dispute arose within the ruling Sindhia family and Britain backed a rival claimant for maharajah in 1843. Known as the Mahratta War, the army of "John Company," fought a bitter conflict which, as Henty said in his preface, enabled the British "although at the cost of much blood, to free a large portion of India from a race that was a scourge—faithless, intriguing, and crafty, cruel, and reckless of life."

The main character of this tale is Harry Lindsay, the son of a British officer and his wife who are murdered. The baby is whisked away by a faithful ayah and brought up as an Indian. Able to speak the Mahratta language and understanding the political nuances of the local government, Harry is singled out for special assignments after he joins the Company army. Traveling to Malaya, he is involved in the cession of Singapore, and on his return to India is thrown into unplanned adventures in the Andaman Islands in the Sea of Bengal. Harry is with the army as they fight the decisive Battle of Maharajapore and in the end sails back to England to claim his legacy.

WITH MOORE AT CORUNNA

(1808)

Napoleon dethroned the incompetent king of Spain and gave the Castilian crown to his own brother Joseph. Spain and Portugal rose in revolt and the English government sent prompt aid to the insurgents. For the next five years, British armies operated in Spain and Portugal in the Peninsular Campaign. The redcoats followed Sir Arthur Wellesley, later known as the Duke of Wellington, in battle after battle with the forces of Napoleon. General Sir John Moore commanded the English army but was killed in action at Corunna fighting a successful rear-guard action.

We are introduced in this story to a character who appears in three Henty volumes on the war in Spain: Terrence O'Conner, son of an officer in the "Mayo Fusiliers." The lad is an underage ensign but he wades into battle early at Rolica and Vimiera in Portugal. He rides into Spain on the staff of General Fane with the invasion force of Sir John Moore. Forced to retreat by the action of the great French General Soult, Moore faces about to fight at Corunna. Though a victory for Moore, the British continue the retreat without Terrence. The Irishman leads a band of Portugese irregulars, rescues his cousin from a convent, and is at the fall of Oporto.

THE YOUNG BUGLERS

A Tale of the Peninsular War (1810)

Sir Arthur Wellesley and other generals welded together English, Portugese, and Spanish troops into an effective fighting force that stymied Napoleon's Marshals for five years on the Iberian Peninsula. The French were forced to send thousands more men to Spain than they could afford and the genius of Wellesley kept them on the run or in unfavorable tactical positions, frustrating all the finely crafted plans of the Emperor.

This exciting book was the first boys historical novel by G.A. Henty and remains one of the best. The heroes are brothers Tom and Peter Scudamore who leave school upon their father's untimely death. Their tenure with relatives is short-lived as they run away to enlist and are shipped out to Portugal and Wellesley's army. The experiences of the two heroes provide a Baedeker of battles on the Peninsula and their exploits inbetween lure any reader into the story. The boys escape from every danger and are recognized for their boldness and bravery.

EUROPE
ABOUT 1812
Scale of Miles
100 50 0 100 200 300

The Napoleonic Empire
Vassal states of Napoleon
State allied with Napoleon

Longitude West from Greenwich 0° Longitude East from Greenwich 10° 20°

GOLDSCHMIDT & HAMPEL, N.Y.

UNDER WELLINGTON'S COMMAND

A Tale of the Peninsular War (1809-10)

Wellington assumed overall command in 1809 with a total strength of about 25,000 men. As Sir Arthur Wellesley, he had served in India for ten years and had fought in the earlier campaign in Portugal. Although the French had a quarter of a million men under arms, they were fighting in hostile country and had to be disbursed to maintain control. Their supply system was not up to the job. The two armies clashed at Talavera (after which Sir Arthur was awarded his peerage and became the Duke of Wellington), Busaco, Albuera, El Bodon, and others until 1814 when the Peninsular War ended.

Once again, Terrence O'Connor is in the field, now a colonel and spoiling for a fight. He is captured at Talavera but escapes and makes his way across France eventually rejoining his Portugese irregulars known as the Minho Regiment. Throughout the campaign, Terrence carries on a correspondence with his cousin Mary waiting for him in Ireland. He protects noble Spanish families in the fall of Ciudad Rodrigo and loses his leg in a gallant action in the Battle of Salamanca. Invalided out of the army, Colonel O'Connor retires to his estate in Ireland and weds Mary.

THROUGH RUSSIAN SNOWS

A Story of Napoleon's Retreat From Moscow (1812)

Exasperated with Czar Alexander's duplicity, Napoleon moved on Moscow with a 500,000 man army. He defeated the Russians at Borodino and marched triumphantly into the deserted capital in September of 1812. There the French waited for five weeks for the Czar's capitulation, a surrender which never came. Three-fourths of the city burnt down, the French supplies ran low, and the agonizing march home began. The ice and snow of winter, starvation, and the Cossack raiders decimated the Grand Armee and less than one fifth of the original invasion force survived. General Winter had defeated Napoleon as it had Charles XII, and as it would do to Hitler 130 years later.

Henty gives us two brothers as heroes, Frank and Julian Wyatt from Weymouth. Julian, through some fault of his own, is carried to France by smugglers and ends up in a French prison. Given the opportunity to fight for France in Germany, Julian agrees and is off to the invasion of Russia where he sees combat at Smolensk and Borodino and faces the horrible retreat from Moscow. In the midst of the terror and death of the march, he rescues a child of a Russian nobleman and is suitably rewarded. Brother Frank obtains a commission in the army in England, learns Russian, fights a duel, and is sent on detached service to Russia as aide-de-camp to Sir Robert Wilson. The Wyatt brothers meet in St. Petersburg, exchange stories and return to England where prosperity and vindication await.

ONE OF THE 28TH

A Tale of Waterloo (1815)

The armies of the Duke of Wellington and Emperor Napoleon Bonaparte finally met in the cataclysmic and decisive Battle of Waterloo in Flanders. Wellington's coalition command numbered about 67,661 on the field, of whom 32,000 were British; the French forces numbered 71,947 men. When the smoke cleared, 22,100 British and Prussians and about 25,000 French lay on the field, dead or wounded. About 8,000 French soldiers were prisoners. People of the time and historians since then have seen it as a turning point in history—Napoleon was exiled to Elba and relative peace descended on Europe until the war in the Crimea 40 years later. Napoleon had changed the map of Europe and the world.

This story is essentially an adventure story which brings the hero to Waterloo in the end. Captured fairly early on by a Dunkirk privateer, Ralph Conway is carried off to the West Indies from where, after various adventures, he enlists in the 28th Regiment with his friend Stapleton. They fight in Ireland and then embark for the Continent under Wellington. At Waterloo, Ralph loses an arm and settles down to claim the estate left to him in a will, the subject of the first half of the book. Waterloo was so important, every survivor was awarded a commemorative medal and that single day of combat was worth two years service on military pension.

INDIAN
TROUBLES

--- ✠ ---

1820 - 1840

WITH COCHRANE THE DAUNTLESS

A Tale of the Exploits of Lord Cochrane in South American Waters
(1820)

Admiral Sir Alexander Cochrane fought with great distinction throughout the Napoleonic Wars. His squadron chased French fleets and patrolled the Caribbean. Although he was described as an extraordinary seaman and was known as an officer who hauled in exorbitant amounts of prize money, the controversial and somewhat eccentric Cochrane criticized the Royal Navy and disgraced himself several times. Always combative and looking for new ways to win, he even advocated the use of chemicals as naval weapons. Fifteen years after the defeat of Napoleon, the Admiral was out of the Royal Navy and involved in aiding Chile's rebellion against Spain.

The hero of the tale is Stephen Embleton who joins the merchant marine and seeks adventure in the Malay archipelago. He accompanies the remarkable trouble-magnet Cochrane to South America where he is captured by the Spanish and, of course, escapes, only to barely survive a series of adventures down the Amazon. Arriving in Brazil he discovers the ubiquitous Cochrane embroiled in the rebellion against Portugal. All comes right in the end and Stephen ends up back in England a rich man.

ON THE IRAWADDY

A Story of the First Burmese War (1824)

British missionaries and merchants had long suffered from the hostility of the Rangoon government and by 1824 the situation had become unbearable. Sir Archibald Campbell mounted a punitive expedition against the Burmese, capturing the capitol and the city of Prome. Having settled the matter of British rights to trade, he was appointed governor of a British administration in Burma.

In this account of the First Burmese War, Stanley Brooke joins his merchant-uncle in Burma but drops everything to participate in the campaign. Traveling through the jungle, he rescues two men from a leopard, joins a band of marauders, and becomes the local law enforcer in conquered territory. Stanley rescues his kidnapped cousin, makes a spirited defense at an abandoned monastery, and then rejoins the army for the last fights with the numerically superior Burmese army. The action takes place in the jungles along the Irawaddy River and when the shooting ends with British victory, Stanley returns to England and the offices of a prosperous trading enterprise.

In Greek Waters

A Story of the Grecian War of Independence (1821-27)

Fed up with centuries of Turkish domination, the Greeks joined in the spirit of the times by rebelling and seeking independence from their Muslim overlords. At the brink of losing the lopsided struggle, Greece attracted the support of Russia, who saw an opportunity to bash the Turks; Britain, who saw the noble and romantic heritage of the ancient Greeks fighting for survival, and France who did not trust the other two and was always looking for influence in the Mediterranean. Not permitting too much autonomy however, the powers imposed a monarchy on the hapless but newly independent Greeks.

Herbert Beveridge is an independently wealthy "philhellene" who, with his sailor-son Horace, acquires a boat and sails to join the Greek rebellion. Discovering to their horror that Greeks and Turks slaughtering each other is unpleasant indeed, the father-son team seek to use their schooner, newly named Misericordia, to aid victims of both sides in the struggle. After several harrowing adventures, Horace is captured by the Turks and sent to Constantinople to await his fate. Rescued before the Sultan decides which appendage to detach first, Horace and his father sail away, disabused of the romance of the rebellion.

WITH THE BRITISH LEGION

A Tale of the First Carlist War (1835)

When King Fernando VII died in 1833, his little daughter Isabel was proclaimed Queen and his widow, Maria Christina, assumed power on her behalf. The king's brother Don Carlos claimed legal right to the throne based on an ancient Salic law prohibiting female succession. War erupted between the "Carlists" and the "Cristinos." The traditionalist challengers were centered in the mountains of Northern Spain and fought a prolonged guerilla war against the supporters of the Queen Regent, including her ultimately successful army.

Henty untangles the complexities of the Carlist struggle through the life of Arthur Hallett. He enlists in a British force known as "the Legion" and sails off to fight in Spain. After some hard fighting, the Legion disbands, but Arthur remains on as British representative in the capital. Dangerous adventure dogs his trail as he seeks to be a moderating influence between the contending forces for whom cruelty seems second nature. True to form, he marries a Spanish heiress and takes her home to a peaceful and prosperous end.

To Herat and Cabul

A Story of the First Afghan War (1840)

Throughout the 19th century, the British and Russian Empires vied for ascendancy in the Middle East, especially Persia, Afghanistan, and India. Like moves on a chess board, the two super-powers played "The Great Game" with the native peoples as pawns. The British decided to put their choice for leader, Shah Shuga, on the throne in Kabul. The ousted shah, Dost Mohammed and his son Akbar Khan determined to play the game by their rules and they proved themselves fierce pawns indeed. Because of a series of crises instigated by the Afghan tribes, the British were forced to leave Kabul with about 4,500 troops and 12,000 women and children and other camp followers. The entire column was destroyed piecemeal, and only one man, a Dr. Bryden made it to the fort of Jallalabad in India to tell the tale of the greatest military disaster suffered by the British in that century.

Angus Cameron, the hero of this book, was captured by friendly Afghans and compelled to witness the calamity. His whole story is an intensely interesting one, from his boyhood in Persia, his employment by the government in Herat, and the defense of that town from the Persians. Angus is always at the point of danger, and whether in battle or hazardous expeditions, he shows how much a brave and resourceful youth can accomplish, even against so treacherous a foe as an Afghan bandit.

THE VICTORIAN ERA: DEFENDING AN EMPIRE

--- ✠ ---

1850 - 1900

THROUGH THE SIKH WAR

A *Tale of the Conquest of the Punjab* (1850)

The British determined to secure their borders with Afghanistan as a result of the First Afghan War disaster. The Kingdom of Lahore proved to be disinclined to cooperate. It was the land of Maharaja Ranjit Singh, who had used the militant Sikh religion "as an instrument to forge a common identity among his followers" (Knight, p. 74). He recruited European mercenaries to train his army and he had the foresight to maintain good relations with the East India Company. Upon his death and because of the recent destruction of the British Kabul army, the Sikh generals persuaded the new leaders to mount an attack on a Company provincial outpost in December of 1845. The resulting war was fought in European style with two tough veteran armies. General Gough led the British in "a series of brutal slogging-matches" in which they lost 2,400 men but prevailed in the end.

Percy Graves goes to the Punjab to join his uncle, an adventurer serving Ranjit Singh. Percy helps defeat a small army sent to destroy his uncle's fortress. He then joins the Company's army to fight the Sikhs and serves heroically in the desperate charges against the well-defended fortresses and professionally served artillery of the Punjabi warriors. With the defeat of the Sikhs, he takes up a career in India and sees action again in the Great Mutiny a few years later.

JACK ARCHER

A Tale of the Crimea (1854-56)

The Crimean War was the first major war among Europeans since the days of Napoleon. It exposed to the world the need for changes in the British military. Tsarist Russia had long threatened the Ottoman Empire, always zealous to acquire access to the straits into the Mediterranean from the Black Sea and hungry for political hegemony in the Balkans. A quarrel between Greek Orthodox and Roman Catholic monks in 1853 over Jerusalem holy sites led to other disagreements and eventually to armed conflict between Russia and Turkey. The British and the French determined to come to Turkey's aid, choosing to make their demonstration in the Crimean Peninsula by capturing the Russian-held port of Sevastopol. The muddled campaign which followed demonstrated the tactical inadequacies of the old generals and made the whole situation unnecessarily deadly due to the total breakdown of allied logistics. Because of the horrible conditions in Scutari, where Henty himself served, 8,000 British troops died in the first four months. In the end, the Tsar died, Sevastopol fell, and peace was restored.

Jack Archer begins the tale as a midshipman in her Majesty's Navy and survives some excitements on the way to the Crimea. As a landsman, Jack takes part in or witnesses the Battles of Alma, Balaclava, and Inkerman, and eventually the fall of Sevastopol. Before the final victory, he is made a prisoner and billeted with a Russian family whom he helps out of a tight spot but then has to flee. Escaping to Poland, Jack links up with partisans fighting the Russians, leaving them to finish of the war in the Crimea.

IN TIMES OF PERIL

The Great Indian Mutiny (1856-59)

India was the linchpin of the British Empire. Controlled by the East India Company (called 'John Company' by the soldiers), and protected by the various armies of India, the subcontinent remained relatively peaceful most of the time. Several mutinies by English-trained Indian soldiers called Sepoys occurred over the course of the century, but none compared to the explosion of rebellion in Bengal in 1857. Initially triggered by rumors of English insensitivity to and scorn for both Hindu and Muslim dietary prohibitions, the deep-seated hatred of the Europeans burst forth against both civilians and soldiers—men, women, and children—and they were slaughtered by the hundreds by mutinous soldiers in the cities and cantonments of Bengal. The battles and massacres that followed in Kanpur, Delhi, Meerut, Cawnpore, and Lucknow seared the memories of Englishmen and Indians alike for decades to come. Two years of war quelled the mutiny and the British retribution was ferocious and far-reaching. The administration of India was taken from the Company by the Crown, never to be returned.

Brothers Dick and Ned Warrender, sons of an English officer in India, are seeking adventures and participating in pig-sticking in the cantonments when the Mutiny erupts. They join the battles around Delhi, survive the massacre at Cawnpore, and endure the siege of Lucknow. They survive the rebellion and return to England unscathed. It is a harrowing tale of treachery and heroic last stands.

RUJUB THE JUGGLER

(1856)

This is the second Henty volume dealing with the Great Mutiny in India. It was published in the United States under the title *In the Days of the Mutiny*. As the rebellion spread, isolated English and loyal Indian survivors withdrew to strongholds to fight off the sepoy attackers and pray for the arrival of a relief column. Lucknow was the most famous siege that resisted to the uttermost and was saved by the arrival of the evangelical Christian General Henry Havelock.

The hero of this tale is Ralph Bathurst, a district officer who is trapped in a besieged English community but is branded a coward because of his fear of the noise of gunfire. After escaping the encirclement, he is attacked again and the girl he loves is captured and put in possible thrall to a wicked Rajah. With the help of Rujub the juggler, he rescues her, overcomes his fears, and escapes to freedom and matrimony.

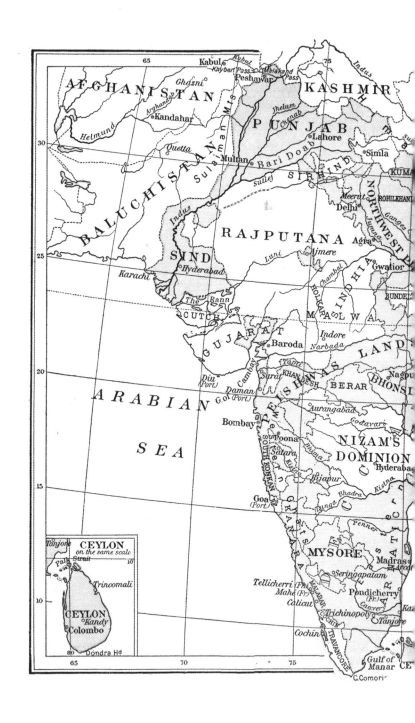

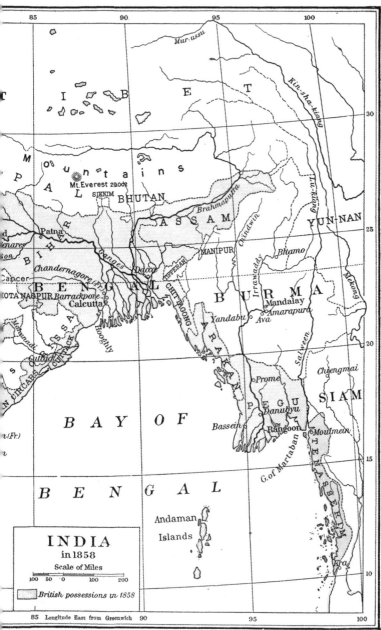

85 90 95 100

Mur-ussu

I B E T

30

M o u n t a i n s

PA L Mt.Everest 29.002
SIKKIM BHUTAN
ASSAM

Brahmaputra

YUN-NAN

25

Patna MANIPUR Chindwin Bhamo

BIHAR Ganges Dacca

Chandernagore (Fr.)

Capcer

KOTA NAGPUR Barrackpore
Calcutta Hooghly

B E N G A L

CHITTAGONG

TIPPERAH

B U R M A

Mandalay
Amarapura
Yandabu Ava

ARAKAN

Irrawaddy

Mahanadi Cuttack

N CIRCARS

(Fr.)

Salween

Chiengmai

20

Prome

P E G U
Danubyu

Basseín Rangoon Moulmein

SIAM

TENASSERIM

G.of Martaban

B A Y O F

15

B E N G A L

Andaman
Islands

INDIA
in 1858
Scale of Miles
100 50 0 100 200

British possessions in 1858

Kra

10

85 Longitude East from Greenwich 90 95 100

GOLDSCHMIDT & HAMPEL N.Y.

WITH LEE IN VIRGINIA

A *Story of the American Civil War* (1861-65)

Few wars have been fought out by each side with greater intensity of conviction of the rightness of its cause or with more abundant personal heroism than the American War Between the States. Virginians initially voted not to withdraw from the Union, but the threat of invasion by the new armies of Abraham Lincoln convinced the men of the Old Dominion to change from reluctant unionists to rabid secessionists and join their sister states of the deep South. The newly minted Confederate men of Virginia armed themselves and prepared to defend their homes.

In this heroic clash of opposing conviction, Henty tells the story of a young Virginia planter, Vincent Wingfield, who, after bravely proving his sympathy with the slaves of brutal masters, serves with great courage and enthusiasm in Jeb Stuart's cavalry under Generals Robert E. Lee and Stonewall Jackson. He has many hairbreadth escapes, is several times wounded and twice taken prisoner. His courage and readiness and, in two cases, the devotion of a black servant and a runaway slave whom he assisted, bring him safely through all difficulties. He fights in all the major campaigns of the Army of Northern Virginia and becomes one of the few escapees from Elmira Prison. Young Wingfield, who is conscientious, spirited, and "hard as nails," would have been a man after the very heart of Stonewall Jackson.

OUT WITH GARIBALDI

A Story of the Liberation of Italy (1862-65)

Giuseppe Garibaldi ranks with Mazzini and Cavour as the third in the great triumvirate of Italian liberators. In his twenties, he fought in the rebellions against Italian tyrants and was sentenced to death for those activities. He fled to South America and fought for the liberty of Rio Grande del Sul against Brazil and of Uruguay against Argentina before returning to Italy in 1848 where he again backed a losing cause. Ten more years of exile and adventure brought him back to Italy for the final time. A real-life Henty hero, Garibaldi led his volunteer army of 1,000 "red shirts" against 100,000 men and defeated the Kingdom of the Two Sicilies in 1860. He fought the forces of the papacy one more time and retired and became a farmer. He was elected to the Italian Parliament in 1874 and died in 1882.

Henty followed the great Italian patriot in the field for a London newspaper and this book is based on his own experiences. The English hero is Frank Percival, the son and grandson of English supporters of the Italian struggle for freedom who joins in this multi-generational insurgence. Frank joins the forces of Garibaldi in search of his fathers who are prisoners of the Neopolitan government. His adventures in Italy lead him to the battles against Sicily and the rescue of his kin.

THE MARCH TO MAGDALA

(1867)

This is not a boys adventure book but a straightforward account written by Henty for London papers and magazines of the British Abyssinian Campaign of 1867-1868, led by Lord Napier. This was Henty's second book, and as Special Correspondent, he gave excellent descriptions of the army and its foibles, the terrain and environment, and the culture of the tribal inhabitants during the arduous 400-mile march.

The Abyssinian monarch, Tewodros, known to the Europeans as Theodore, had imprisoned a number of British subjects and seemed to have relished the opportunity of testing Her Majesty's soldiers in combat. He awaited their arrival in the mountain fastness of his capitol 15,000 feet above sea level. General Robert Napier led his army of India and 50 elephants, more than 7,000 camels, 13,000 mules and ponies, 7,000 bullocks, and 13,000 sheep across a waterless desert. After an artillery bombardment, and amidst thunder, lightning, and rain, the storming parties rushed to the walls and gates of the city where they planted their ladders and battled their way into the city. A private and a drummer scaled a cliff and fought hand to hand to enter the city first, both being awarded the Victoria Cross for their gallant action. King Theodore, "Lord of the Earth, King of Kings, Saviour of Jerusalem," was killed on the ramparts, brave to the last.

MAORI AND SETTLER

A *Story of the New Zealand War (1870)*

The indigenous Maori people of New Zealand were courageous and resourceful fighters and they resisted English settlement from the 1840s to the 1870s. Their land was mountainous and forested and their individualistic guerrilla style and ability to adopt European weapons made them a formidable foe. Ambushes, night attacks, and hand-to-hand fighting with tomahawks and knives struck fear in the hearts of young British soldiers. Often, Maori women fought like demons when the English settlers encroached on their land and the British soldiers were appalled by the distaff warriors' willingness to die in battle. This is a straightforward account of the Hwa rebellion.

The Renshaw family emigrates to New Zealand and faces numerous adventures on the long crossing. Wilfred, a strong, self-reliant, courageous lad is the mainstay of the household. He has for his friend Mr. Atherton, a botanist and naturalist of herculean strength and unfailing nerve and humor. The majority of the text covers the long trip out and the skirmishes with savages of Tierra del Fuego and the South Pacific. There are many breathless moments when the odds seem hopelessly against them but the British survive and prevail. When peace is restored, Young Wilfred becomes an important character in the colony and settles in one of New Zealand's pleasant valleys.

A WOMAN OF THE COMMUNE

(1870)

This is the only Henty book published under five different titles: *A Girl of the Commune*, *Cuthbert Harrington*, *Two Sieges* and *Two Sieges of Paris*. The Franco-Prussian War provided the setting for this rather complicated tale of intrigue involving various proto-feminists in the Paris Commune. A series of international intrigues between France and Prussia over the throne of Spain led to a French declaration of war. The French had a courageous army, but one which was obsolete in weapons and tactics. Napoleon III and his second-rate ministers proved to be no match for the efficient military machine of the Kaiser and within six weeks, the emperor surrendered a force of 86,000 men at Sedan and a month later, another 175,000 men at Metz, after their virtual destruction on the field of battle with the Prussians. Paris and Napoleon's government fell, and the Franco-Prussian War made Germany a unified empire and France a republic.

Cuthbert Hartington, a son of a squire of Abchester, is studying painting in Paris when the war erupts. He joins with the French forces and faces the might of the new Prussian army. He falls in love with one of the daughters of a solicitor from his home-town who has cheated Cuthbert's father out of his estate. After confronting the persecutor of his family and settling matters by forcing restitution, he then shows grace toward his enemy. He returns to Paris and becomes embroiled in the Paris commune where a left-wing art student, Minette, is taken and executed. Upon returning to England, Cuthbert marries Mary, now somewhat cured of her feminism, an ideology opposed by Henty.

THE YOUNG FRANC-TIREURS

Their Adventures in the Franco-Prussian War (1870)

This is one of Henty's first books and is based on his experiences covering the Franco-Prussian War as a correspondent and from interviews he conducted with French veterans. The background to the war is explained above in *The Girl of the Commune*. The humiliation of the defeat and the loss of Alsace-Lorraine remained in the minds of the French people for 44 years and in 1914 they again hurled the flower of French manhood against the Germans in World War I. Together the two nations lost more than 3,000,000 killed.

The heroes of this story are Ralph and Peter Barclay who live in their mother's city of Dijon. When war is declared, they join the French forces and see action against the Prussians. They need adventures to avoid becoming casualties in this war. They enter Paris in disguise, they swim the Seine in winter, and they finally escape in a balloon, the first and last of Henty's heroes to get away by that means. Upon their return to England, the boys enter respected professions and, a Henty rarity, remain unmarried as the story ends.

BY SHEER PLUCK

A Tale of the Ashanti War (1873)

The "Gold Coast" continued to provide trading partners for England long after the slave trade ended in the early 19th century. The Fante tribe lay between the Ashantes and the coast, and when the Ashantes attacked those intermediaries, the British under General Sir Garnet Wolseley led the 23rd, 42nd, and 95th Regiments (later to become the Royal Welsh Fusiliers, The Black Watch, and Rifle Brigade) on a punitive expedition. Hacking their way through dense jungle, the British, uniformed in loose-fitting grey uniforms, worked their way to the tribal capital of Coomassie. The guerilla warfare encountered on the march changed to pitched battle and the cannibals were driven from their city. Four Victoria Crosses, England's highest combat honor, were won on this campaign. G.A. Henty and Henry Morton Stanley also took part as correspondents and were actually involved in the fighting. Imagine the skirl of bagpipes resounding from the steaming, dripping, pestilential jungle as the Highlanders charged through the bush.

Frank Hargate accompanies a professional naturalist, Mr. Goodenough, to West Africa where they experience dangerous adventures in their search for new flora and fauna. In this most deadly of environments, long known as "the white man's grave," the naturalist fails to cope with such adversity and dies. Frank is detained by the chief but escapes before he could become another one of the human sacrifices that littered the Ashanti capital. He follows the British expedition that had been so carefully planned by General Wolseley and sees it through to the capture of Coomassie.

THE MARCH TO COOMASSIE

(1873)

This book is a compilation of Henty's dispatches to London during the war with the Ashanti. In that short but arduous campaign he describes his harrowing trip up the Volta River in Henry Morton Stanley's *Dauntless* and the enormously difficult march to the enemy capital. Henty freely describes the various African tribes, both allies and enemies, and their particular cultural affectations. British officers come in for criticism or praise, and he especially singles out the Control Department for inefficiency in transport and supply. Henty expounds on the medicinal value of rum and tobacco as defenses against malaria. The main engagement at Amoaful is a first person account full of details of heroism and suffering; the average British soldier acquits himself bravely and receives high praise. The Ashanti were a formidable enemy on their own terrain and the additional allies of malaria, jungle rot, heat stroke, and exhaustion make the success of this little war an amazing achievement. The Ashanti themselves, while brave and aggressive, are nonetheless bloody savages who practice human sacrifice and live in utter moral darkness. As in *The March to Magdala*, this Henty title is military journalism at its best.

FOR NAME AND FAME

With Roberts to Kabul (1878)

The British and Russians were both zealous to gain representation in the Afghan court in the 1870s. A Russian representative was welcomed to Kabul in 1877 but the British were, at the same time, denied diplomatic access. A British ultimatum was refused and the "Great Game" entered its next phase in the Second Afghan War. Sir Frederick Robert's "Kurram Valley" column, one of the three sent against Kabul, experienced marked success and established General Roberts as the leading British officer in India.

The main character of the story is Will Gale, who was kidnaped by gypsies and raised in a workhouse in England. Shipping aboard a merchant ship, he experiences several adventures among the Malays until ship-wrecked off the Indian coast. Upon arrival in Calcutta, he enlists in the British 66th Regiment leaving to join General Roberts. Showing a natural intelligence and exhibiting uncommon valor, Will rises quickly to the rank of captain. He is wounded and taken prisoner at Peiwar Kotal but escapes to join in the final defeat of Ayoub Khan. In a campaign short on luxury and long on suffering, Will is rewarded in the end with the discovery that his father is Colonel Ripon of his own regiment, and he who was lost is now found.

THE YOUNG COLONISTS

A Tale of the Zulu and Boer Wars (1879-81)

The Zulus had emerged in the 19th century as one of the most powerful tribes in Africa. Their territory lay on the eastern coast of southern Africa, adjacent to British-held Natal and the Dutch Boer republics. Peaceful relations between Britain and the Zulus prevailed for 30 years until 1879, when the English embarked on territorial expansion. The British High Commissioner, expressing the need to protect the Transvaal from Zulu encroachment, sent British into Zululand for a quick and painless conquest which turned long and bloody. At Isandlwana, a British column of 1,300 men was wiped out by the Zulu Impis. In 1880, 7,000 Boers rose in rebellion against the British and declared the independence of the Transvaal. The Boers were a courageous and virile people. In the battles at Laing's Nek and Majuba Hill, the Boers, also known as Afrikanders, mauled the British army and were granted autonomy as the South African Republic.

The hero of the tale is full of "pluck and daring," but Henty criticizes the British tactics and, in his introduction, "found it painful to describe these two campaigns in which we suffered defeat." Dick Humphreys and his friend settle with his family in Natal and go along with the British column into Zululand. They are on a ridge outside the camp at Isandula (Isandlwana) and have a ringside seat of the British defeat. After a few days of hunger, they surrender to a Zulu band, but escape. After several adventures, the boys get caught up in the Boer conflict and witness the disasters at Laing's Nek and Majuba Hill. They go home in disgust over the war's outcome.

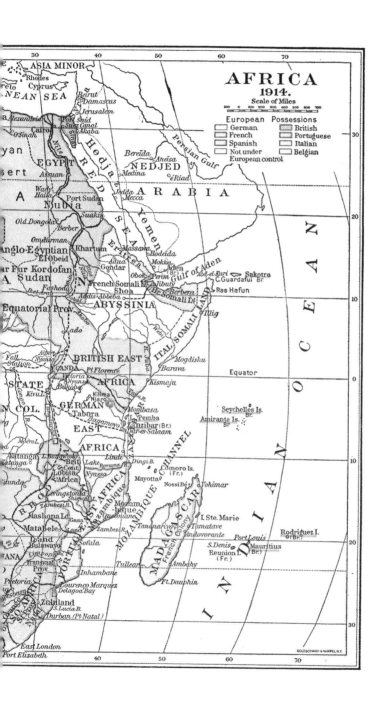

A CHAPTER OF ADVENTURES

The Bombardment of Alexandria (1881-82)

This title was published in the United States as *The Young Midshipman*. As a tributary of the Sultanate of Turkey, Egypt had managed to operate with great independence under the extravagant and clever Khedive Ismail. The large debts incurred by his government increased every year, worrying the British investors in the Suez Canal. Britain and France forced Ismail's abdication and placed several of their own men in the cabinet of the new khedive. In 1881, a charismatic colonel of the Egyptian army, Ahmad 'Urabi led a rebellion of Egyptian nationalists against the new regime; Britain ordered out the troops to help the new ruler, Tawfiq. In the climactic battle of the campaign, the British army under Sir Garnet Wolseley defeated 'Urabi at Tel-el-Kebir, sent him into exile in Crete, and secured continued British control of the Canal and influence over the Egyptian government.

Jack Robson is a midshipman aboard a merchant vessel bound for Egypt. After his arrival in Alexandria, the city which guards the Suez Canal, he and two fellow sailors get caught up in the anti-British riots and are held as hostages as the Royal Navy bombards the city. As Arabi Pasha's rebellion spreads, the stranded boys escape and join the forces of Lord Charles Beresford who is determined to restore law and order. Following the mopping up operations, Jack makes his way to India and ends the story as a second mate.

THE DASH FOR KHARTOUM

A Tale of the Nile Expedition (1884-85)

The mysterious Nile River and the vast deserts which surround it became the staging area for a Sudanese Arab messiah, Mohammed Ahmad ibn al-Sayyid Abdullah, fortunately known as the Mahdi, who led his followers on jihad against the Egyptian rulers of the Sudan. The British government sent Colonel Charles "Chinese" Gordon to help evacuate Egyptian officials from the capital at Khartoum. Colonel Gordon was an evangelical Christian of great fortitude, conviction, and resourcefulness who had fought the African slave trade as hard as he had fought foreign enemies on the field of battle. "Gordon's story was taken up by the British press, and he became a public hero, the epitome of British pluck and defiance, a lonely figure standing resolutely on the palace roof, scouring the desert through his spy-glass for signs of relief" (Knight, p. 218). Too late came the help: Khartoum fell, 11,000 were put to the sword, including Gordon.

This exciting tale features two brothers, Rupert and Edgar Clinton, whose births get mixed up and they are raised as if brothers by a well-off infantry captain. Edgar runs off to the army thinking he is the adopted son and ends up as a trumpeter in a regiment in Egypt bound for the relief of Gordon in Khartoum. Rupert, in the meantime, has also joined the army and is in Egypt. Edgar is in a flying column crossing the desert. He is soon after captured and enslaved by a Kaffir and survives several perilous adventures. Rupert fights the Mahdi's men from a steamer on the Nile as the rescue of Gordon precedes on that front. Edgar escapes and is reunited with his brother.

THROUGH THREE CAMPAIGNS

A Story of Chitral, Tirah, and Ashanti (1895-97)

Britain fought a number of brush-fire wars that involved one brief campaign or battle. Chitral was a mud and timber fort only 80 yards square in one of the mountainous northwest frontier provinces of India. The British interfered with the nomination of a new king and the tribesmen laid siege to the small British, Sikh, and Kashmiri garrison.

A rebellion by fierce Pathan tribesman brought Lt. Gen. Sir William Lockheart's British army of 44,000 troops. The men of Her Majesty's forces brought their own tribesmen: "The earliest heroes of the campaign were the Gordon Highlanders. Those fierce fighters led the charge that regained the heights of Dargai with 500 highlanders rushing up the 300 yard glacis slope fully exposed to fire. . . . The Highlanders' piper, one Findlater, both legs shot from under him, played 'Cock o' the North' sitting down during the 40 minute battle" (Farwell, p. 323). Byron Farwell called it "one of the most magnificent charges in British military history" (Ibid.).

The Fourth Ashanti War brought the British to Coomassie one more time, hacking their way through dense jungle to fight stealthy warriors who melted back into the tropical rain forests only to hit and run the next day.

The hero of all three tales is Lisle Bullen who is orphaned when his soldier-father is killed in action in a battle in India. After enlisting, Lisle sees action at the Chitral fort and in Tirah against the Pathans. The young infantry officer finally sees service against the Ashanti and in the course of his valorous conduct, he becomes the only Henty hero to win the DSO and the Victoria Cross.

WITH KITCHENER IN THE SOUDAN

A Story of Atbara and Omdurman (1896-98)

Twelve years after the death of Charles Gordon at Khartoum, the British were again roused to reconquer the Sudan. General Sir Herbert Kitchener advanced his 18,000 English, Irish, Scots, Egyptians, and Sudanese into Dongola and defeated Mahdist forces at Firket and Atbara. The final showdown occurred at Omdurman on the Nile when the Dervishes attacked behind their colorful banners in a "triumphant, annihilating charge," neither giving quarter nor expecting any (Ibid., p. 233). The British blasted the Mahdist ranks, dropping them in swaths on the hot sands. When the end came, about 11,000 men in patched robes lay dead with thousands more wounded. The Sudan was retaken by the British. Kitchener was a national hero. Sir Winston Churchill, a veteran of that fight, wrote that Omdurman was "the last link in the long chain of those spectacular conflicts whose vivid and majestic splendor has done so much to invest war with glamour. . . . Cavalry charged at full gallop in close order, and infantry or spearmen stood upright in ragged lines . . ." (Churchill, p. 171).

The hero of the tale is 16-year-old Gregory Hilliard who lives with his widowed mother, the wife of a soldier who disappeared on the relief expedition to Khartoum. He is with Kitchener on the campaign to defeat the Khalifa and takes part in the defeat of the Mahdists at Abara and the destruction of their army at Omdurman. Gregory discovers that his father did not die in the Hicks Pasha massacre as originally thought, but escaped to Khartoum to perish with Gordon. Upon his return home, he claims an aristocratic legacy.

WITH BULLER IN NATAL

or, A Born Leader (1899)

Henty penned this book in the midst of the Boer War, a complicated and unpopular conflict in English history. He confined his story to the fighting in Natal where the British forces were led by the renowned veteran, Sir Redvers Buller, VC. The war between Britain and the Boers of the Transvaal was fought over the English encroachment on the property of the "Outlanders" where gold had been discovered. The diamond magnate Cecil Rhodes financed a raid on the Transvaal by a Dr. Jameson. President Kruger stocked up on modern European weapons for his splendid army, where every soldier was a trained horseman, an accurate marksman, and a fanatical enemy of the British. After Britain rejected demands for withdrawal of forces on the border, the Boers struck. Within a month, the main British force was besieged in Ladysmith. General Buller landed with several thousand troops (eventually British forces numbered more than 500,000!) and marched inland. He suffered heavy casualties at Colenso and disaster at Spioenkop as the sharpshooting Afrikanders fought like lions protecting their lairs.

Chris King is a young man from Johannesburg who leads a band of scouts for Buller in Natal. He and his men creep in near the Boer camps and spy on the enemy positions, they set ambushes and engage in fire-fights, and they dress in farm clothes to go behind the Boer lines. Chris fights at Colenso, is wounded and captured, escapes, and is in on the fight at Spion Kop. The young scout has several more adventures before helping in the final breaking of the siege of Ladysmith. The story ends but the war continues.

WITH ROBERTS TO PRETORIA

A Tale of the South African War (1900)

Field-Marshal Lord Roberts, the veteran of campaigns in Afghanistan and India, relieved Buller of command and directed the second part of the Boer War, the highlights of which were the relief of the siege of Kimberly, the capture of General Piet Cronje's force at Paardeberg, and the capture of the capital of the Transvaal, Bloemfontein. Lord Roberts' assessment of the strategic situation was flawed: "He was a highly successful imperial general, with the tactical and diplomatic skill, and the limitations born of 40 years' peace and war in India. He had no insight into South Africa, knew nothing of the complexity of colonialism, nothing of the tenacity of Afrikaner nationalism, and the extraordinary resilience of the Boer—hunter and hunted, fighting animal and political animal" (Pakenham, p. 398). The war continued as Boer guerillas hammered at British patrols and the 35,000 South African troops still in the field held out to the end.

The young hero is Yorke Harburton who takes passage to South Africa seeking employment after his family's fortune took a turn for the worse. When war with the Boers heats up, Yorke joins Lord Robert's army as a scout in a volunteer unit. As a Dutch-speaker, he slips into Boer towns to gather intelligence. He takes part in several sharp actions (all actions with the Boers are sharp) and his shrewdness and bravery get him more assignments behind Afrikaner lines. He takes messages into the besieged town of Kimberly and is captured by and escapes from a Boer commando. Yorke takes part in the relief of the town, the capture of General Cronje, and the relief of Mafeking.

WITH THE ALLIES TO PEKIN

A Tale of the Relief of the Legations (1899-1900)

Due to the weakness of the Chinese empire, various world powers established "spheres of influence" in the coastal cities of China throughout the 19th century. A common hatred of the "foreign devils" motivated several anti-western societies to rebel, the most successful and violent of which was the "The Patriotic Society of Harmonious Fists," known in the west as the Boxers. They fomented a rebellion which resulted in the murder of hundreds of foreigners, especially missionaries, merchants, and civil servants, and their families. A unique international force was assembled to march on Peking and relieve the foreign legations who were heartily resisting a Boxer siege. The punitive expedition included British, French, German, Russian, Japanese, and American troops, and they fought a pitched battle with the Chinese and rescued the legations. After looting the demoralized city and exacting a huge indemnity, an "open door" policy for trade with China forestalled a general partitioning of the ancient kingdom.

The hero of this tale is Rex Bateman, the son of an English merchant at Tientsin. He is a clever lad who speaks Chinese and is not afraid to take risks. He rescues two cousins whose missionary parents have been murdered and gets them into Peking where about 500 westerners with five cannon and inadequate food will be holding on by a shoestring till help arrives. Rex's adventures lead him to his home city and more fighting until he links up with the disunited international force struggling to reach the besieged foreigners in the capital. After a valiant two month defense, the legations are saved.

ADDENDUM AND
BIBLIOGRAPHICAL NOTES

It is important to note that the Henty books contain illustrations by some of the best illustrators of the age. Pictures fire the imaginations of children and their judicious use can help bring the text alive. The most common Henty illustrators were Gordon Frederick Browne, William I.R. Rainey, and Wal Paget. Leonard Ashley has compiled a list of at least 37 others who contributed to the Henty volumes and Peter Newbolt discusses each of them in his encyclopedic *G.A. Henty, 1832-1902, A Biblio-graphic Study.*

The following is a brief list of works cited in the text or useful for further background. For the collector of Henty, Peter Newbolt's volume mentioned above is indispensable. The Henty Society, an international group of Henty aficionados, publishes an annual newsletter and gathers periodically to discuss his books and ideas.

WORKS CITED

Ashley, Leonard R.N., *George Alfred Henty and the Victorian Mind*, London, 1999.

Berlyne, Gordon, OBE, *Hugh Pruen's Henty Companion*, The Henty Society, 1997.

Bryant, Arthur, *Years of Victory, 1802-1812*, London, 1944.

Churchhill, Sir Winston S., *My Early Life: A Roving Commission*, New York, 1930.

Farwell, Byron, *Mr. Kipling's Army: All the Queen's Men*, New York, 1981.

Farwell, Byron, *Queen Victoria's Little Wars*, London, 1973.

Fenn, George Manville, *The Late G.A. Henty*, London, 1903.

Fuller, J.F.C., *A Military History of the Western World*, New York, 1955, 3 vols.

Gershoy, Leo, ed., *A Survey of Western Civilization*, 4th edition, New York, 1969.

Keegan, John, *The Face of Battle*, New York, 1976.

Knight, Ian, *Marching to the Drums: From the Kabul Massacre to the Siege of Mafeking*, London, 1999.

Larson, Laurence M., *History of England and The British Commonwealth*, New York, 1924.

Motley, John Lothrop, *The Rise of the Dutch Republic*, New York, 1898, 4 vols.

Myatt, Frederick, *The British Infantry 1660-1945: The Evolution of a Fighting Force*, Dorset, 1983.

Newbolt, Peter, *G.A. Henty 1832-1902: A Bibliographic Study*, Scolar Press, Aldershot, 1996.

Packenham, Thomas, *The Boer War*, New York, 1979.

Schama, Simon, *Citizens*, New York, 1989.